"THREE WEEKS AGO, ONE OF OUR MOST CELEBRATED AMBASSADORS DISAPPEARED . . .

"Eight days ago, intelligence reports placed him on Romulus—and I assure you it's an unauthorized visit."

Picard gazed at Admiral Brackett patiently, waiting for her to continue. She moved toward his desk and quickly activated the computer console there.

"A defection?" he queried, in the most even of tones.

"If it is, the damage to Federation Security would be incalculable." Brackett tapped a few more times and then gestured for him to look at his monitor. "Taken on Romulus, by long-range scanner," she said.

The computer whirred and blurred images began to come into focus. The peripheral images were fuzzy, but the central figure gradually came into sharp relief.

Picard found himself looking at the unmistakable image of Spock of Vulcan—dressed in Romulan clothing.

Spock, a revered figure in Starfleet history. Spock, the renowned ambassador. Spock, venerated architect of peace in the galaxy.

Was he a defec

Picard stared a

Look for STAR TREK Fiction from Pocket Books

Star Trek: The Original Series

Star Trek: The Next Generation

STAR TREK®
THE NEXT GENERATION™

UNIFICATION

A Novel by Jeri Taylor
Based on the two-part television episode
Story by Rick Berman and Michael Piller
Part One Teleplay by Jeri Taylor
Part Two Teleplay by Michael Piller

POCKET BOOKS
New York   London   Toronto   Sydney   Tokyo   Singapore

An *Original* Publication of POCKET BOOKS

POCKET BOOKS, a division of Simon & Schuster Inc.
1230 Avenue of the Americas, New York, NY 10020

STAR TREK is a Registered Trademark of
Paramount Pictures.

This book is published by Pocket Books, a division of
Simon & Schuster Inc., under exclusive license from
Paramount Pictures Corporation.

ISBN: 0-671-77056-X

First Pocket Books printing November 1991

10 9 8 7 6 5 4 3 2 1

Printed in the U.S.A.

For Jennifer

ACKNOWLEDGMENTS

Faced with this task for the first time, I now understand how these sections sometimes go on for pages. I hope to compress these expressions of appreciation and hope that the recipients understand that the act represents no dwindling of my gratitude.

To my bosses—Rick Berman, for daring to believe that someone could hold down a full-time job and also write a novel in a month, and Michael Piller, for being ever-present in my head, asking, "Did you find the truth in the scene?"

To my colleagues, Ron Moore, Joe Menosky, Brannon Braga, and Naren Shankar, for support, faith, and love.

To Eric Stillwell, Rick Sternbach, Mike Okuda, Richard James, Jim Mees, Richard Arnold, and Guy Vardaman, for input.

To my wonderful assistant Lolita Fatjo, for holding me together.

To Dave Stern, who asked only, "Have you ever done anything like this before?"

To my mother, for telling me all my life that I was a writer.

To my father, for sharing his love of science fiction.

ACKNOWLEDGMENTS

To my children, for enduring a month of conversations which consisted entirely of discourses on Spock and the Romulans.

To my beloved husband, for saying, every night, "I'll do the dishes—you go ahead and write."

I thank you with all my heart.

Chapter One

ADMIRAL RUAH BRACKETT had a secret.

Not a terribly profound one, and nothing that would ever interfere with her duties as a fleet admiral of Starfleet Command. But it was a secret nonetheless and she enjoyed keeping it. There was something titillating about indulging a private idiosyncrasy that was known to no one.

She felt a momentary twinge of guilt as she and her young aide strode into the transporter room of Starbase 234, for her mission was of such importance that she should not be thinking of her personal pleasures. The message she carried had been deemed too important to risk on subspace and was to be delivered only in person. The security of the Federation might be at stake—and yet the foremost thought on her mind was her anticipation of the next few moments.

"Well, Lieutenant, shall we do this?" She addressed her young aide, Severson, who was looking a little pale under the freckles which dusted his face. Lieutenant Severson, she knew, wasn't looking forward to the experience of transporting from starbase to starship; he claimed it was altogether unpleasant and in fact made him queasy. He suffered it stoically because as her aide there was no way to avoid the process, and after having garnered this plum assignment, he wasn't about to risk it because of transporter nausea.

"Yes, Admiral." He waited until she had taken her place on the pad, then stepped on beside her. They made an unusual pair—the tall, regal admiral with her close-cropped brown curls and the smaller, carrot-headed young man—but in fact they worked effortlessly together, and for that Brackett was willing to tolerate his frailty with the transporter.

"Let us know when you're ready, Chief," she said to the transporter engineer, a seasoned veteran from the planet Nason Barta. He was remarkably fast at entering molecular codes because of the ten digits on each of his appendages.

"I am prepared, Admiral Brackett. Please give me your command."

Brackett smiled. The moment was here.

For the secret was that she *loved* being transported. She knew most people found that it produced no response whatsoever, physical or emotional; others, like Severson, became queasy or disoriented and felt it actively unpleasant.

For Brackett, it was a transcendent experience. The conversion of her molecular structure into a subatomically dissociated matter stream created a sensation that was rapturous: a mystical-spiritual-sexual experience all wrapped up in one powerful phenomenon. Her consciousness remained intact during the transport, of course, and in that breathtaking instant of dematerialization and materialization she sensed that she brushed against something unknowable, some mysterious, powerful force that existed only in that brief and sublime moment. She often felt she was a breath away from grasping, from understanding it—but then it was over and she arrived at her destination. And always, she longed for the next time.

"Thank you, Chief. Proceed."

Severson tensed beside her, and Brackett closed her eyes, focusing on the intense experience that was to come. A roaring sound in her ears signaled the beginning of the dematerialization process, and there was the brief, flashing swirl of light and then the sensation of swooping into a void—then blackness.

A second, a fraction of a second—how long was it? Majestic feelings overwhelmed her; was she soaring? Tumbling? Ascending? There it was, that unknowable something; she was reaching out for it, a second more and she would touch it . . .

"Welcome aboard the *Enterprise,* Admiral Brackett. It's good to see you again."

She looked into Miles O'Brien's cheerful Irish face and smiled automatically. It seemed as though she were swimming up from a dark crystal pool, and she preferred to remain within its remarkable depths. But of course she had business to attend to.

"And you, Chief O'Brien." She looked around Transporter Room Three, still light-headed, getting her bearings. And there was Picard.

She smiled as she saw the familiar face. Jean-Luc Picard was an incredibly attractive man with handsome, chiseled features; he had some time ago lost his hair, except for a closely trimmed fringe around the sides, and as far as she was concerned the baldness added to his virile image. She admired and respected him—but she was also deeply drawn to him on a feral, primitive level. Maintaining the bearing and reserve of a superior officer was always difficult around this man, though she was sure he was unaware of that fact.

"It's good to see you again, Captain."

"And you, Admiral Brackett."

"Shall we?" she asked, and he gestured her ahead of him through the transporter room door; they exited, followed by Severson, who was as pale as a ghost and drawing deep breaths of air to keep from throwing up.

When they had reached the bridge and entered the captain's ready room, she turned to Severson. "You're excused, Lieutenant." The matter she had come to discuss was not for anyone's ears but Picard's.

The captain moved toward his replicator. "Would you care for refreshments? Tea, perhaps?"

She smiled. She knew this man, knew what was going on inside him, knew what he was truly feeling in spite of his remote, detached manner.

"You're a cool one, Picard," she said.

He turned to her, quizzical, an eyebrow lifted, his look asking the question for him.

"I know you well enough to know that you're burning with curiosity about this summons of mine. And yet you almost manage to convince me that your only concern is a cup of Earl Grey."

"And I know you well enough to know that you'll only tell me what you want to in your own good time. So we might as well have tea."

She smiled as he held her look. They were old friends; they'd had these fencing matches many times before. In fact their first encounter—when they were both cadets at Starfleet Academy—had been on the debate team. They delighted in opposing each other with vehement arguments, and then switching sides and going at it again. During the course of their careers they had continued the friendly rivalry and Brackett always found herself looking forward to the match.

So if Jean-Luc Picard wanted to pretend nonchalance, she understood the gambit. But she held the upper hand this time; she knew the startling reason for this meeting, and perhaps she would make him wait for a few moments before she revealed it.

"I apologize for the mystery, Captain," she began, "but we must attempt to contain the information I'm about to reveal to you—at least as long as possible."

He regarded her calmly, waiting with no perceptible indication of curiosity.

"Three weeks ago, one of our most celebrated ambassadors—an adviser to Federation leaders for generations—disappeared. He left no word of his destination."

And still he waited, gazing at her patiently. She moved toward his desk and quickly activated the computer console there.

"Eight days ago, intelligence reports placed him on Romulus—and I assure you it's an unauthorized visit." She keyed an instruction and then said, "Computer, initiate linkage between this terminal and Starbase computer system alpha-two-nine."

"Linkage complete," responded the computer voice pleasantly.

Brackett busied herself for a moment with computer instructions, wondering if Picard would interject a question. When he did, it was minimal. "A defection?" he queried, in the most even of tones.

"If it is, the damage to Federation security would be incalculable." She tapped a few more times and then gestured for him to look at his monitor.

A blurry image appeared on the computer screen— it seemed to consist of several figures but none was distinguishable. Picard leaned in, trying to decipher it.

"Taken on Romulus, by long-range scanner," said Brackett. "Computer, enhance image in section four-delta."

The computer whirred and the blurred images began to come into focus. The peripheral images were still fuzzy, but the central figure gradually came into sharp relief.

Admiral Brackett looked for Picard's reaction as he found himself looking at the unmistakable image of Spock of Vulcan—dressed in Romulan clothing.

Spock, a revered figure in Starfleet history. Spock, the renowned ambassador. Spock, venerated architect of peace in the galaxy. Was he a defector to the Romulans?

Picard stared at Brackett in astonishment, and she could not resist a wry smile.

At least now she had his attention.

Chapter Two

COMMANDER WILL RIKER was so wrapped up in his thoughts as he strode the corridor of Deck Eleven that he ran right into Ensign Gretchen Naylor. Their shoulders bumped and he snapped out of his reverie to find the tall brunette with pale green eyes looking at him in surprise.

"Excuse me, sir, I should have been more careful—"

"It's my fault, Ensign. I was a million light-years away and I wasn't watching where I was going. You okay?"

"Just fine, sir." She smiled and held his gaze with her amazing eyes, and the tall, bearded officer found himself wondering if Ensign Naylor had engineered this little mishap. He realized he had been noticing her quite a bit lately, though always in the most innocuous of circumstances. She had been in Ten-Forward, the ship's lounge, a few times when he was there, and in Engineering when he had held a consultation with Lieutenant Commander Geordi La Forge. She wore a gold uniform and might be assigned to any area of ship's operations; he realized he had no idea what it was she did.

"What's your post, Ensign?" No reason not to familiarize himself with the crew of the ship; that fell well within his duties as first officer. It was only Naylor's green eyes and her generous, full-lipped mouth that made him feel as though this were a more personal inquiry.

"Security, sir. I work with Lieutenant Worf in R and I—recon and intelligence." Her smile was direct and straightforward, lacking any hint of innuendo. Riker liked that smile. His mind shot forward to the two of them in Ten-Forward, heads bent together in quiet conversation, Naylor's mouth parted as she listened, little tendrils of dark hair falling forward as she leaned toward him . . .

"Very well, Ensign. Carry on." Riker heard himself dismissing her and saw a momentary flicker of something—disappointment?—in her eyes. He nodded and walked on, wondering if she stood and stared after him, perplexed by his abrupt departure. He didn't look back to find out.

Now was not the time to indulge in a shipboard flirtation. He knew himself well enough to know that his feelings were particularly vulnerable at this point, and an innocent friendship might rocket out of control. That was dangerous on a starship, a small community where everyone knew everyone else. An intense love affair could go wrong, leaving an uncomfortable residue; on a ship millions of light-years from port such a situation could create the kind of friction that spread like the Circassian Plague and undermined morale and efficiency. Riker had learned iron self-discipline in order to avoid such troublesome situations.

For he was feeling restless again. That was the most precise term he could find for the vague miasma that overcame him from time to time. It wasn't intense, it wasn't dire, it wasn't profound. Just unsettling.

The first thing he always noticed was a slight tendency to become distracted. Sitting on the bridge, hearing the routine cadence of orders given and received, he would find that he had missed a few minutes of activity because his mind was in an Alaskan wood, hearing the crunch of his footsteps on icy snow.

Craving for certain foods was another symptom. He would be almost overcome by longing for hot oatmeal with cinnamon, a bubbling potato casserole, or steaming split-pea soup—all warm, filling dishes that his father used to make on cold winter nights.

And then, inevitably, his mind would turn to thoughts of his own command.

It was a matter Riker thought he had resolved, and it annoyed him that it kept creeping back, like an irritating sound that can't be completely blocked. His decision to stay on the *Enterprise* as first officer was a conscious choice that completely satisfied the rational part of his mind. His reasons were sound and he had comfortably come to terms with them.

Why, then, this nagging refrain? Why this occasional lapse into introspection and doubt? Riker liked tidiness in his life, and this refusal of his feelings to be neatly compartmentalized distressed him.

What he needed was an adventure. His *own* adventure. They were even now racing through space toward Vulcan, hoping to discover the events leading up to Ambassador Spock's strange disappearance. But that was the captain's mission, and though he would do everything he could to support and abet that mission, it was not his.

Riker stopped outside Holodeck Two, his mind still tumbling with these unwelcome thoughts. The holodeck had been his destination, for he often came here when he was feeling restless, and usually found some measure of satisfaction in an hour or two of music. Music had the power to quiet his mind, to restore his serenity, and to rejuvenate his enthusiasm. It made the difference in his life.

What program would he choose tonight? He'd often lost himself for hours playing trombone with a simulated New Orleans jazz group. But ever since the appearance of the remarkable female holofigure Minuet in that program—and her reemergence in the elaborate scheme of the alien child Barash—the purity of that music had been compromised.

"Earth," Riker found himself saying after he had keyed instructions to the holodeck computer. "Memphis, Tennessee. Year, 1925. A honky-tonk called Stumpy's."

"Program complete," came the dulcet tones of the computer, and the doors to the holodeck slid open.

The noise and the smoke greeted him immediately. The babble of happy voices was welcoming; the smoke not so. It was necessary background for a bar on Earth in the twentieth century, of course, and holodeck technology had long ago found the means to re-create the smoky atmosphere without injecting dangerous particulates into the air. Still, Riker found it incomprehensible that people long ago had systematically occluded their lungs with the foul-smelling stuff and considered it a mark of sophistication.

He walked into Stumpy's—a tiny place crowded with tables—and saw a room of smiling faces turn toward him. There were welcoming calls and a smattering of applause and encouragement as Riker walked toward the piano standing on a makeshift platform.

"Willie . . . tinkle them things, Willie . . ." This from a gravel-voiced black man with white tufts of hair over each ear.

"They'd rather hear you, Stumpy." Riker smiled at him. "I'm not in your league."

"Naw, naw . . . you got the licks, man."

Riker sat down at the piano and let his hands drift over the keys for a minute, getting his bearings, letting himself absorb the atmosphere. This was where the blues was born, and he was now a part of that energy and excitement, the unique creativity that spread throughout the South of the United States in the early part of the twentieth century.

His hands came down on the keys and the patrons of Stumpy's became quiet. Riker started slowly, gently, letting the music come from inside, not imposing anything but simply letting it happen. His pain, his restlessness became part of the music and were lifted out of him and into the air of the funky little club in Memphis. The people listening absorbed the music, sensed the intensity of the feeling within it, let it wash through them and reflected it back until everything was one huge, shared experience, music and hurt, music and longing, music and aspiration turning and twisting with one another—

"Captain to Commander Riker."

Riker opened his eyes as the clipped tones intruded into the holodeck. It was always the rudest of awakenings, the invasion of the outside into the fantasy experience, but it was the price one paid for serving on the *Enterprise*.

"Freeze program," he instructed the computer, and the patrons of Stumpy's became instantly stilled. He touched his communicator. "Riker here, sir."

"Could you join me in the conference lounge?"

"Right away, sir." Riker rose from the piano and cast one last glance around the honky-tonk. So much for the restorative powers of music. He would summon the discipline to function as he must, providing his best to his captain.

Of course, there was always the possibility that the captain's summons might signal the beginning of an adventure. *His* adventure. Something difficult and mysterious that would test his mettle, summon his talents and hone them in rarefied challenge.

There was a new spring to his walk as he left the holodeck and hurried toward the turbolift, contemplating these possibilities.

But the next hour with the captain was spent helping him trace through intelligence reports detailing Ambassador Spock's last two decades of activity. Negotiations, mediations, arbitrations—there was a well-chronicled history of Spock's ceaseless efforts as an architect of peace. If there were seeds in his public behavior of a defection to the Romulans, they were well buried.

Riker enjoyed these meetings with the captain. He respected the well-honed process that Picard brought to any endeavor: Picard would examine thoughts, tumbling them around in his mind like a gem polisher, extracting something here, buffing something there, until he could put them all together into a codified whole. It was always stimulating, and always challenging, to interact with him.

But it was a demanding process. Riker stretched his legs and then looked at the captain, realizing that he had been at this for hours even before Riker arrived. Weariness hung over Picard like a veil. "We'll be coming into orbit around Vulcan in less than an hour, sir," Riker said. "You may want to get some rest."

"Yes, yes, of course, you're right." But he didn't move. Riker saw the captain's eye caught by another padd on the table, and knew that, although Picard was tired, his mind was still churning.

"We should notify Sarek's wife of our plans," suggested Picard.

"All taken care of, sir. She'll be waiting for your signal to transport on board." Riker had talked with Perrin, Sarek's human wife, by subspace.

"And Sarek?"

"She says he is too ill to join her."

"Not unexpected. The man is dying." There was an undertone of sadness to the words. Riker recalled the meeting of those two several years ago, when Sarek, suffering from the rare affliction Bendii's syndrome, came aboard the *Enterprise* and created havoc by inadvertently projecting his emotions onto the crew. Riker almost smiled as he remembered himself and the captain snapping and snarling at each other, and the patrons of Ten-Forward engaging in a barroom brawl. The outcome of that experience, of course, had been a mind meld between Sarek and Picard, which allowed the venerable ambassador to maintain control of his emotions long enough to complete an important negotiation. The mind meld had linked Sarek and Picard in extraordinary intimacy, and Riker had no doubt that the captain was carrying some residual effects of that liaison.

"And I have the . . . honor," Picard continued, "to bring him the news that his son may have betrayed the Federation."

Riker sensed, from instincts developed after long association, that the captain wanted to talk further. He needed a sounding board to reflect his thoughts and feelings. It was a role Riker played comfortably and well. "How well do you know Spock?" he asked.

He waited patiently as Picard rose from the table and paced toward the windows, gazing at the spectacular sweep of the stars as the *Enterprise* raced by them at warp speed. "I met him only once. What I know of him comes from history books and of course the mind meld with his father."

"That must cover a lot of ground." Riker couldn't imagine what a mind meld would be like, but it had to have given the captain a source of insight into Spock.

But the captain smiled wryly, and said, "Not as much as you'd imagine. Sarek and Spock . . ."

He hesitated, and seemed reluctant to go further. Then he looked at Riker and said, simply, "Well, sometimes, fathers and sons . . ."

"Understood," answered Riker. He knew Picard was aware of his own tortured history with his father. He had no difficulty imagining other strong-willed men having similar difficulties. But he couldn't help but wonder what problems of Spock and Sarek the captain was privy to.

Picard finally rose, and Riker was glad he was

taking the time for a break before they reached Vulcan. They were at the door when Picard suddenly turned back, as though remembering something, and picked up a padd.

"There was one other thing," he said. "Take a look at this."

Riker took the padd and scanned its contents briefly as Picard continued, "Something that turned up during the intelligence sweep on Spock. What do you make of it?"

Riker absorbed the succinct report. "Metal fragments, possibly disassembled components, identified as Vulcan—recovered from a downed Ferengi ship . . ."

"And the crates they were in were marked as medical supplies."

Riker raised an eyebrow. "Contraband?"

Picard simply shrugged his shoulders as he started toward the door. "They've been sent to Vulcan for identification. Starfleet has requested we lend them a hand."

And he was gone.

Riker stood in the empty room, holding the padd in his hand, rereading the information, hoping to discover in it something that promised an adventure.

But all he saw was a mundane investigation. Identifying metal fragments. Hardly the stuff to challenge the mind and electrify the sensibilities. But it was better than nothing.

Chapter Three

JEAN-LUC PICARD SMILED as he entered Transporter
Room Three and saw Miles O'Brien at his post. He
liked O'Brien immensely. O'Brien was the kind of
man who wore well, like old leather, becoming more
comfortable over time. Picard had seen him move
from amiable bachelor to loving husband and now,
within recent weeks, to fatherhood. Molly Miyaki
Worf O'Brien had been born in Ten-Forward during a
catastrophic event on the *Enterprise,* and Picard was
sure that O'Brien's life was now topsy-turvy. In fact,
as he approached the ruddy, curly-haired transporter
chief, he was sure he could see dark circles under his
eyes, testifying to lack of sleep.

"Hello, Chief. How are Keiko and the baby?"

"Very well, sir. Molly's got an Irish set of pipes,
that's for sure. And she uses them, all night long."

"I thought you were looking a little peaked."
Picard's warm smile eliminated any hint of chastise-
ment.

"It's amazing to me, sir. She seems to wake up the

minute I go to bed. She sleeps soundly all day long, never fusses, nurses well. But no matter what time it is I try to go to sleep, she starts squalling. Do you think they do these things on purpose?"

Picard had no idea what babies might or might not do and had no particular interest in finding out. Babies were strange, burbling little creatures that others might enjoy fawning over; he was content to observe them from afar. "I'm afraid I'm not the right person to ask, Mr. O'Brien," he responded. "You might speak to one of the pediatric nurses."

"Oh, I'm not complaining, sir. I think she's just being a baby. And I wouldn't have it any other way."

"Is our guest ready to come on board?" Enough of this talk of babies; he was here for a purpose, one that had galvanized his energies as no mission had in a long while. Visions of Spock haunted his mind and invaded his dreams. He had become possessed by the mystery of Spock's disappearance in a way that was overwhelming and disturbing. And he had no doubt that it all had to do with his mind meld with Sarek.

"Aye, sir, I can bring her on any time."

"Then let's do it."

Picard moved toward the transporter platform as O'Brien keyed commands into his console. There was a brief silence, and then the sparkling effect of the transporter beam began to form on the platform and coalesce into a woman's body.

An instant later Perrin stood before him, lovely and gracious as ever, her graceful features tranquil and composed. Only her eyes mirrored the pain she carried from dealing with Sarek's illness.

"Captain Picard." She walked toward him, two arms extended. Her warm, honey-blond hair was artfully done, as always, and her hazel eyes radiated compassionate gentility.

"Perrin." He lifted his hands and she grasped them firmly, pressing a generous greeting.

"It's good to see you again."

"And you. How is Sarek?"

Her face clouded slightly as they moved toward the door of the transporter room. It was a remarkably expressive countenance, the play of her emotions reflected in subtle ways, like the drift of sunlight and shadows on an ever-changing sea. Living with a Vulcan must have taught her control, and there was always a certain reserve to her behavior; nonetheless her humanness had not been suppressed, merely distilled. Picard had found her, from the moment he met her, an enchanting woman. So much so that he dared not think of her often, and then only with the firm reminder that she was wife to Sarek. And to what extent these feelings resulted from his mind meld, he was not at all certain.

"Sarek has good days . . . and bad days. More and more they're bad."

They exited into the corridor and proceeded down the corridor toward a turbolift.

"Then the disease has progressed?"

"It is a cruel killer. Sarek deserves a noble death. Instead, he is trapped in this lingering madness."

"It must be very hard for you." When he uttered those words, Picard saw Perrin's head swing around to him. He realized that she was unused to anyone thinking of her feelings, her needs, and was caught somewhat off guard. She was silent for a moment before she responded.

"Every day I can share with him is a gift. The pain will be in losing him."

"I hope that time will not be soon."

"There's no way to tell. At times I think he won't make it through another night, and then it seems he's strong enough to live for years."

The two walked quietly for a moment, Picard heavily aware of her presence next to him, catching a faint scent of something fresh and floral. His next words came out unbidden, as though they had somehow bypassed his conscious mind. "Perrin, I admire your strength more than I can tell you."

Again, he felt her sidelong glance, but he was careful to keep his eyes trained straight ahead. She did not respond, and the two walked the rest of the way in silence.

Perrin stared out the windows of the conference lounge at the dusky red of the planet Vulcan. She had traveled in space many times, but was always struck by its awesome beauty. It was cleansing, she thought, to view her world from above; it changed perspective and allowed her to free herself for a while of the burdens that afflicted her when she was on the surface.

Burdens? Had she thought that word? How had it crept into her mind? A wave of guilt swept over her for an instant as she acknowledged that Sarek's illness had become a burden to her. He was her husband, she loved him beyond all things, she owed him so much— she mustn't think of his dreadful malady as an encumbrance.

It was Captain Picard's unexpected solicitude that had triggered these feelings, she was sure. His caring statement, acknowledging that the situation was difficult for her, had tapped into emotions that she had tried hard to keep quiescent, and now, as if through a tiny hole that keeps ripping larger, everything was trying to spill out. Well, they might try, but she would push those feelings right back where they belonged. She had become good at that.

"Perrin?" Picard's voice caused her to spin around, and she saw him standing before her with two cups of steaming tea. She smiled and took one, deeply inhaling the vapor.

"Mint tea—it's been years since I've had it. Vulcans have some strange concoction they call 'mint,' but you wouldn't recognize it." She sipped at the fragrant liquid and turned back to gaze out at the stars. If only she could stand there for hours, sipping this lovely tea and gazing at the glories of space . . .

"Perrin, you know why I've come to Vulcan." Picard's voice was gentle, but it grated on her nonetheless. She knew the purpose of this visit and she had no desire to go into it. She knew it was inevitable and that the captain didn't have the luxury of avoiding it. Still, it was so calming just to look out, see Vulcan as a huge orb, hazy and florid, just one planet among millions and millions.

"I must ask you about Spock."

Now she turned, bitter feeling welling up in her, threatening to overcome her precarious control. "He didn't even say good-bye to his father before he left." She saw Picard's warm eyes gazing at her, saw his instinctive understanding of her feelings, his effort to make this easier for her. She was grateful.

"Is it possible he was abducted?"

"No. He wrapped up his affairs very carefully. He

knew he was going." Looking back, in the weeks since his disappearance, Perrin had realized what a calculated move Spock's departure had been. His estate, his lands had been provided for in the form of a manager; his diplomatic functions had been brought to resolution. It made his behavior even more reprehensible to her.

"Do you have any idea why he might have disappeared like this?"

Perrin drilled him with a look. How could one ever know why Spock did anything? A more closed and private man she had never met. Sarek, by comparison, was voluble and communicative. She strained to keep her voice dispassionate as she answered. "Captain, as far as I'm concerned he disappeared a long time ago."

She saw Picard's surprised look and realized the bitterness in her voice had suggested more harshness than she intended.

Everything had been difficult about her relationship with Spock, right from the beginning. She had frankly not been prepared for life among the Vulcans. She thought she knew them well; at Skidmore University in upper New York State, she had Vulcan friends and always found their cool reserve comforting. Her own mercurial personality was balanced by the unflappable calm of her Vulcan companions, and she found it a pleasurable combination.

She was still not prepared for the impact of Sarek upon her life. She had traveled to Vulcan as a youthful historian, eager to become his amanuensis. The morning she met him she fell in love with him, a great lion of a man, powerful and urgent. That he apparently felt the same way about her still seemed a miracle.

When she married Sarek, his son Spock was approximately four times her age.

She had no idea what Spock thought about her. He was polite, solicitous, and deferential. He could not be faulted for any of his behavior toward her. Yet for all she knew he might loathe her, so absent of any emotion was he in her presence.

Did he feel resentful that she had taken his mother's place? Amanda had died years before, in old age—her human life span woefully shorter than the Vulcans'. Any child feels the loss of a parent, and Perrin feared she might be the natural recipient of any residual feelings Spock might be carrying about the absence of his mother. She had even tried to talk to him about it, hoping to clear the air and pave the way for a relationship that was comfortable, if not warm. But Spock had shut her off, clearly unwilling to discuss such intimate matters with her—politely, of course, but definitively. It was the last time she tried to have a personal conversation with him.

She could never even define the role she might play with him. "Stepmother" seemed almost grotesque for a child so much older than she. "Friend" had seemed a worthwhile goal, but she felt Spock precluded that. In the end, there was no definition that suited whatever it was they were to each other; she was simply Sarek's wife.

But when Spock had disappeared, a wellspring of anger within her was tapped. For she was left behind to see what that unexplained departure had done to Sarek.

As though reading her mind, Picard turned back to her and said, "Would it be inappropriate to ask what happened between you and Spock?" She stared at him, emotions surging, wondering if she should simply stay silent and leave. Much more of this and she would be in tears. She drew hard for air.

"Not between us. Between Spock and his father. They had argued for years; that was *family*. But when the debates over the Cardassian War began, he attacked Sarek's position—publicly. He showed no loyalty to his father." It had been a terrible time. It all came back to her now, Sarek's quiet pain, his refusal to condemn his son, her own anger toward Spock.

"I was not aware," said Picard carefully, "that Sarek was offended by Spock's position."

"*I* was offended. And I made sure Spock knew it." Had she been wrong to do that? Had she in some way even widened the break between father and son? She had tried to temper her response, even then, but every time she saw Sarek's wounded eyes, her fury rose anew. "I am very protective of my husband. I do not apologize for it."

A silence hung in the air. Picard apparently decided to move away from that charged subject. "Would Sarek have any idea why Spock might have left?" he asked.

And if it were anyone else, she might never have become so personal, so revealing. But talking with this man pulled feelings out of her. "If you could see him as I do . . . wasting in bed . . . whispering to himself . . ." Perrin looked at Picard's kindly face and found it easier to keep going. "He wants to see his son, to heal any rifts that still remain, before he dies. But now it may be too late."

Her voice broke and she turned away, not wanting to reveal the extent of her anguish. And yet, it felt a little better, now, having said even that much to

Picard. She heard his compassionate voice behind her and knew he had been sobered by her distress.

"Perrin . . . would you allow me to see Sarek?"

She turned back to him, assailed by a welter of uncertainties. Did Picard have any idea what he was asking? Could he know how fervently she had protected Sarek from outside eyes? How could she add to her husband's humiliation by allowing him to be viewed by others? And yet . . .

"If it were anyone else, I would never permit it." She stepped forward, studied his eyes. "But you are a part of him, and he of you."

She turned away, her decision made.

Riker was grumpy.

He stood with Chief Engineer Geordi La Forge in Cargo Bay Two, watching the activity before him, annoyance curling every nerve ending in his body. Spread out before them on the floor of the huge bay were sections of metal—big ones, small ones, damaged, immaculate, irregular, symmetrical—a hodgepodge of shards and chunks and fragments. It was a metal mess.

"The Vulcans can't figure out what these fragments are," he told Geordi, "but they've identified the metal as a dentarium alloy."

"That pretty well indicates that they're Vulcan," replied Geordi. "And dentarium also means that whatever this was, it was designed for use in space."

The two surveyed the tangle of metal for a moment. Geordi wore a metallic visor over his eyes; it shone in bright contrast to his ebony skin. Blind from birth, Geordi had undergone an operation in his childhood, which allowed him to "see" through the visor that was directly connected to his visual cortex. "From the look of the damage," he offered, "it must've been a high-speed impact."

Riker acknowledged the observation. "A Ferengi cargo shuttle that went down in the Hanolin asteroid belt. The debris was spread over a hundred square kilometers." None of the Ferengi had survived, of course, or they might not be having to go through this time-consuming procedure. Now all they had was this heap of metal and the intriguing fact that it had been packed in crates marked as medical supplies.

Maybe those were the only crates the Ferengi had on hand at the time, thought Riker, whose interest in this whole affair was waning. He had decided that in his next life he would certainly not become an archaeologist. He simply didn't have the patience for this kind of slow, detailed reconstruction. If there were answers, he wanted them now.

Restless.

Forcing himself to concentrate, he walked along the rows of metal chunks that Geordi and his crew had laid out. He picked up part of a damaged container; Geordi picked up a fragment and played his tricorder over it.

"Could it be a weapons array?" he asked.

"That was my first thought," admitted Riker. "But the Vulcans don't have any record of stolen weapons. Or stolen parts, for that matter. Or stolen anything."

Geordi shook his head as his visored eyes roamed over the vast array of mangled metal parts. "This is going to be like putting together a big jigsaw puzzle—when you don't know what the picture is supposed to be."

Riker nodded, trying to find a way to instill in this

project a sense of excitement. That's when he spotted Ensign Naylor on the other side of the room, studying a padd. Had she been here all along? How could he not have seen her? Was she assigned to this project?

And was this the excitement he was seeking? Warning alarms sounded in his head, and he turned away before their eyes met.

The walk through Sarek's mountain estate had been calming. It was designed to be just that, Picard knew, with its carefully planned landscape of off-world plants and hybrids. As soon as he had passed through the wall (most Vulcan homes were walled, a practice Picard personally thought somewhat medieval) he was greeted by the sight of formal gardens, their orderliness imparting a sense of tranquility. Fountains dotted the grounds, their gentle sounds creating a graceful counterpoint to the symmetry of the plantings. The arrangement reminded Picard of certain Japanese gardens he had visited, and from which he had always emerged refreshed and pacified.

Of course, on Vulcan, it was beastly hot. He'd been on the surface only minutes and already he could feel perspiration dampening his body. The heat was oppressive, a blast furnace laid open. Perrin, who had greeted him at the gate, looked over at him and smiled in sympathy.

"Awful, isn't it? When I first moved here I had to wear a cool suit. Gradually I adapted, but it's still like living in Death Valley."

She led him through the gardens and into the house, with its spacious, high-ceilinged rooms and sparse furnishings. Vulcans seemed to enjoy concocting elaborate gardens that delighted the eye with pattern and

26

variety, but their homes were as empty of artifact as they could make them. Furnishings were simple and few; adornments were rare. A visit to a Vulcan home was rather like visiting a temple.

As they passed through the halls, footsteps echoing on the slate floors, Picard was aware of people retreating before them like wraiths. Shadowy figures melted into doorways or rounded corners ahead of them. It was, he knew, a Vulcan show of courtesy, of granting privacy to their guest by not intruding on his presence. Still, it was an eerie feeling, as though he were walking through a house haunted by unseen spirits.

Perrin paused before a great carved door—one of the few examples of ornamentation—and glanced over at him. He could see the strain in her face, the apprehension in her eyes as she prepared to usher him into Sarek's chamber. Her eyes implored him for—what? Understanding? Compassion? He returned her look, silently promising whatever she asked.

The door swung open and the two stepped in.

The room was large and airy; walls of windows flooded the room with light. There was one piece of furniture in the room—a huge, raised bed. Upon it lay Sarek. His face was turned toward them but he did not see them; his eyes were turned inward, to some country deep within. Rivulets of tears had dried on his face, and his mouth moved faintly, though no sound emerged.

Picard was shocked at the man's deterioration. When last he had seen the ambassador, he was in the first stages of Bendii's syndrome. His emotions were threatening to break their bounds, but with effort and meditation Sarek was able to achieve a measure of control.

The man on the bed before him had lost that capacity. His white hair was matted and clumped; his strong, angular face was haggard, as though rampant emotion had extracted a terrible toll. His lashes were wet with tears, and his mouth, cracked and dried, moved ceaselessly.

"He's like this most of the time," Perrin said. "His emotions have taken over."

She moved toward the bed, followed by Picard. Picard had the sensation of awful violation. This man Sarek should be remembered as a prince among men—authoritative and substantial. There was something horribly wrong about seeing him in this pitiful condition.

"Sarek! You will listen!" Picard was startled by the demanding tone of Perrin's voice. But it produced an immediate result in Sarek. He snarled in rage, anger rushing to the surface in a volatile display.

"Go from me!" There was certainly nothing feeble about the roar that emerged from his mouth. He was like a wounded animal, furious and lethal.

"Picard is here." Perrin's own voice was strong and unintimidated. In reply, Sarek began pounding his fists on the bed.

"No—more—chaos!" The scream was guttural and anguished, and it sounded in Picard's heart like an iron bell. Perrin looked toward him, face impassive.

"I'll leave you alone. He'll either acknowledge you, or he won't." She turned and left the room, and Picard found himself alone with the aggravated man.

His mind flashed, unbidden, to his first encounter with Sarek, and the extraordinary experience of the mind meld. He could feel Sarek's strong fingers on his face, and the indescribable emotions that overwhelmed him as Sarek's energy passed into him. The hours that followed were harrowing. Rampant emotions swept through him, wave after wave of unbridled passions: anger, sorrow, lust . . . all in a shifting kaleidoscope of sensation, dizzying and dire. It was unbearable, yet inescapable. Was this what Sarek dealt with every moment of his life? How could he not go mad? Picard had never conceived of emotions so compelling, did not know if he could endure them a moment longer . . .

He stared at Sarek still pounding on the bed, mind caught in a fury whose cause was already forgotten. Picard took his cue from Perrin. He approached the bed and spoke with firm authority.

"Sarek, I have come a long way to see you." Those words only seemed to enrage Sarek more. The cords of his neck became distended as he bellowed.

"I will not answer!"

"I must speak to you about your son."

"I want no one with me—"

"About Spock."

Suddenly Sarek went silent. The tension went out of his body and he was very still. Then, slowly his head turned toward Picard and his eyes seemed to focus.

"Spock?" His voice was so quiet Picard could hardly hear him.

"Yes. He's missing."

There was a flicker in Sarek's eyes. Picard hoped he was moving into the reality of the present from wherever he had been.

"Is that you, Picard?"

"Yes, my friend."

Sarek looked at him like a bewildered child.

"You came here . . . to Vulcan . . ."

"I need your help. I must find Spock."

Tears sprang to Sarek's eyes. Picard realized that his emotions were so volatile, so fragile, that they could overwhelm him at any time. A strangled sob emerged from Sarek's throat as he struggled for the control that was so elusive. "He is not here."

"I know. He is reported on Romulus."

Now Sarek's eyes focused on Picard. He was summoning concentration from some reserve deep within; the effort was considerable but he seemed determined to achieve it.

"On Romulus. Why?"

"That's what I hope to find out from you."

"On Romulus."

Sarek fell silent again, as though musing. But this time Picard did not sense a retreat from reality but rather a contemplation of the situation. When he looked at Picard again, his eyes were clear. It was remarkable. Picard was staring not at a feeble old man but at the legendary Sarek, a man in control of his faculties, mind strong and nimble. What did it cost him to achieve that control at this point in his disease?

"You're going there, aren't you?" Sarek queried. "To find him."

"Yes."

Sarek brought himself upright. Purpose had given him strength and it was beginning to course through his veins. Picard felt as though he were watching someone awakening from the dead.

"Have you any idea what might have taken him to Romulus?"

"No."

"Is there anyone on Romulus whom he might know—or choose to contact?"

A vague memory seemed to stir within Sarek. "Pardek," he whispered.

"Who is Pardek?"

"It could be Pardek . . ."

"Who is Pardek?"

Now Sarek was getting out of bed. His robe fell in folds around him, billowing around his legs as he began to pace.

Picard stared at him, not believing this transformation.

"He is a Romulan senator. Spock has maintained a relationship with him over the years. I don't know where they met. The Khitomer Conference, I'd imagine."

"Pardek represented Romulus?"

"Yes. Yes, I'm quite certain he did."

Sarek was striding around the room, leonine and magnificent, as lucid as he had been in his prime. Picard didn't know quite how to handle this situation. He had no idea if Sarek could go on like this for hours or if he might collapse at any moment.

"In fact, I recall Spock coming to me with optimism about a continuing dialogue with the Romulans at one point. And I told him it was clearly an illogical expectation." Sarek smiled slightly and said, as though in an aside, "Spock is always so impressionable."

He walked to his magnificent wall of windows and gazed out at the Vulcan gardens, at the tan-and-ocher sweep of the desert to the red mountains in the distance. "This Romulan Pardek had no support at home. And of course, in the end, I was proven correct."

He turned and looked at Picard with a shrug, as though to say, How do you tell a child what to do?

"I tried to give him the benefit of experience, of logic," he said mildly, "but he never listened. He never listened . . ."

Picard saw Sarek losing the train of thought as though it were a whiff of smoke rising in the air. He couldn't be sure how much more he would get from the man. Clearly his lucidity was fragmentary at best. But he had to try. "It has been suggested that he may have defected."

Sarek fixed him with a stern glare. "Never. I can accept many things, but never that."

"But you believe he might be there to see Pardek?"

Sarek looked puzzled. "The Romulan senator? How do you know Pardek?"

"I've heard of him." Picard figured it wasn't worth trying to retrace Sarek's tortured steps. The old man was nodding, still pacing.

"That's what he's done. Gone to see Pardek."

"Do you know what business they could have together?"

"No." Sarek turned away and walked toward the bed, showing signs of exhaustion. "I never knew what Spock was doing. When he was a boy, he would disappear for days at a time. He would take his pet sehlat, I-Chaya, and climb into the mountains. His mother would be beside herself."

Sarek turned back toward Picard, who couldn't tell if the man was recollecting the past or creating it. But Sarek seemed to have an urgent need to reveal what he was saying.

"I asked him where he had gone, what he did . . . he refused to answer. I insisted he tell me, but he would not. I forbade him to go . . . he ignored me. I punished him . . . he endured it silently. And always, he returned to the mountains."

His eyes sought Picard's. "One might as well tell the river not to flow."

Picard saw that Sarek's eyes were wet once more, tears welling up, threatening to overwhelm him. But still he needed to speak. "Secretly, I admired him . . . that proud core of him that would not yield . . ."

And then he was silent, tears coursing a path down his cheeks. Picard was incredibly moved. It was as though Sarek's anguish were his own, and he was suffering as Sarek suffered. He even felt tears beginning to sting his eyes.

"Sarek, we are a part of each other. I know Spock has caused you pain. But I also know you love him." A cry burst from Sarek at this and he looked imploringly at Picard.

"Tell him, Picard . . ."

Then his eyes began to glaze over slightly, and Picard sensed a slight panic in the man as he struggled to maintain control for a moment longer. He looked toward his hand, lifted it, and tried to form the Vulcan salute. But his fingers wouldn't obey. They trembled and shifted position and refused to go where they should. Gently, Picard reached over to him and put the fingers right. Sarek smiled and held the hand toward him. Picard formed the salute himself.

"Peace and long life, Sarek."

"Live long and . . . and . . ." He stopped, confused, his mind drifting. "Live long and . . ." His voice trailed off vaguely, his hand losing the salute and his mind losing reality. Sobs welled up in him and he turned away, stooped and frail, rampant emotions claiming him once more.

"Spock . . . my son . . ." He cried softly, choking with ineffable sadness and longing.

Picard felt a chill as he watched Sarek cry like a child, the name of his son occasionally punctuating his sobs. He knew it would be the last time he saw this man.

"And prosper," he whispered.

Chapter Four

IT IS WRONG. A lifetime of discipline washed away, and in its place, bedlam . . . nothing but bedlam. And I am helpless to prevent it! I am old! Nothing left but dry bones and dead friends. Weary, so weary . . .

Picard's eyes snapped open and inexplicably he found himself in his own bed in his quarters on the *Enterprise.* His heart was hammering in his chest and he could feel dampness on his cheeks from tears.

Slowly, he sat up, eyes adjusting in the darkness. It was his quarters, all right; the padd he had been using earlier was on the bedside stand where he had left it, with a half cup of now-cold tea nearby. Where had he been in his dream?

The memory was slipping away even now, an elusive wisp dancing just ahead of his grasp. He remembered being cold, unbearably cold . . . there was a sensation of torment and misery . . . overwhelming passions crowding in on him, suffocating him—

Sarek. That was it; he had revisited the mind meld.

Picard sat up in bed, far from sleep now. It was his habit to dissect disturbing dreams like this, to attack them head-on and process them completely. He believed that was the way to deal with these unbidden denizens of the night: haul them up into consciousness, look at them, explore them, probe them, make them such a part of the rational mind that they could never again descend into the depths of the unconscious.

That he was connected to Sarek in some profound, indescribable way he did not doubt. That this connection should invade his dreams did not seem odd. What it portended for his encounter with Spock, should that occur, he did not know. That realization made him uneasy. Picard preferred to feel certainty, and there was almost nothing in this mission that allowed him that luxury. He was afloat in a landscape of strange, mystic possibilities that his mind could not even grasp, much less control. That wasn't the way he liked to do things.

He sat up in bed and reached for the padd. He needed to focus his mind, to deal with realities— things precise and tangible. He worked for a few moments, refining the plan he had concocted. He thought it workable, though risky. The most difficult part of it would probably be in persuading Admiral Brackett to approve it.

But he did have a few ideas about that.

His face on her viewscreen was affable and confident. To Admiral Brackett, that meant he was about to present her with some proposition that was dangerous, unwieldy, intractable—or some combination of all three.

She adored this man.

"Yes, Jean-Luc"—she smiled, in her most earnest manner—"how can I help you?"

"Admiral." He smiled. "I have visited Vulcan, and talked with Spock's father and stepmother."

"Yes?"

"They were unable to give me any real insight into Spock's motives for going to Vulcan. However, I learned from Sarek the name of a Romulan senator with whom he might have been in contact."

"Who is that?"

"His name is Pardek."

"Yes. Pardek."

"You know of him?"

"A senator . . . he has the reputation of being a moderate."

"So I gather."

"Then—you would make contact with Pardek?"

"Yes. Admiral . . . getting through the Neutral Zone and to Romulus is not a simple task."

"Of course not."

"I have a plan, but you will need to approve it."

Every finely honed instinct in Admiral Brackett went on alert with that statement. Even though Picard tried to speak of it casually, this "plan" sounded alarming.

"Let me outline it for you," continued Picard.

"Please don't," replied Brackett.

Picard's face on the viewscreen was quizzical.

"Jean-Luc—I very strongly suspect I don't want to know this plan of yours."

"But, Admiral, I must have your approval."

"You have it."

"Pardon me?"

37

"My approval. You have it."

"I see."

"Any further questions?"

There was a long moment, and Brackett held his look imperturbably. Picard was no fool. He realized that her blanket approval also meant that if anything were to go wrong, she would disavow the entire mission. But she was sure it was the only way she could give him the freedom he needed to complete this most delicate of assignments.

Was that a faint smile she saw on his lips? Maybe, maybe not. But finally, he responded in the most even of tones. "No, Admiral, no more questions. I think we understand each other perfectly."

She nodded toward him and the transmission ended. *Have a safe journey, Jean-Luc. I would miss you terribly if you did not return.*

Picard's spirits lifted as soon as he entered the small, private room just off the bridge that served as his office. He knew there were many on board who were uncomfortable here; it could be a bit claustrophobic, especially when the captain's will (or the captain's ire) was at its most potent. It had been described to him by Will Riker as an experience in which all the available oxygen in the room seemed to have been absorbed by the captain's forcefulness, leaving the recipient literally struggling to breathe. Picard had smiled at this, not displeased,

To him, the ready room was sanctuary. It reminded him of his mother's closet at home in France, near the village of Labarre. He had discovered that room as a very young boy; it was large for a closet, and for some reason possessed a window high on one wall. It provided enough light for reading, and young Jean-Luc would spend hours in there, safely nestled behind the rack of clothing, reading books and fantasizing about his future.

Often, as he hid there, he would hear his father or his older brother, Robert, calling for him. They wanted him to help in the vineyards, of course, but Jean-Luc's dreams were not of earth but of the stars. He would be up there one day, he was sure of it, riding the heavens in a spaceship. What purpose would it serve now to tend the grapes?

His father had plenty of answers to that question, and whenever Jean-Luc reappeared his father would be irate, demanding to know where he had been. But he never told. He would no longer have had his sanctuary if he had.

I asked him where he had gone . . . he refused to answer. I insisted he tell me . . . but he would not. And always, he returned to the mountains.

Sarek's words flashed into his mind and Picard drew an involuntary gulp of air as he realized the parallel. Spock and Sarek, he and his father . . . fathers and sons . . .

The door chimed and Picard was drawn out of his reverie. "Come," he said.

Lieutenant Commander Data entered. "You wanted to see me, sir?" he asked, waiting patiently for the captain's orders.

Picard turned to his second officer. The pale android gazed calmly at him through his golden eyes; Picard realized he had been in a momentary reverie and had quite forgotten that he had requested Data's presence. That wasn't like him. He worked to clear his mind, address the matters at hand.

"I'd like your help, Mr. Data, in preparing for my journey to Romulus."

"I would be happy to be of assistance, sir."

Picard could do all of this himself, of course. But he enjoyed sharing sessions of information retrieval. He often summoned Will Riker for that purpose, and as frequently turned to Data. He found the android officer an ideal backboard off which to bounce ideas, theories, hypotheses. The fact that Data was a synthetic rather than a biological being meant that his responses came uncluttered with human emotion. That gave them a purity of reason that was usually helpful and, on occasion, stunningly insightful.

"I'd like you to access Starfleet records on Romulan legislators."

"Yes, sir. Anyone in particular?"

"His name is Pardek. He's a senator."

"Sir, I believe I know why our messages are not being answered."

Picard frowned slightly at this statement from his Klingon chief of security, Lieutenant Worf, standing now at his tactical station on the bridge. Picard had come to an aft station to review the material Data had accumulated.

For three days now, as they had been warping toward the Klingon home world—the first phase of his plan to get to Romulus—they had been trying to reach Gowron, head of the High Council. In that Picard and his crew were directly responsible for Gowron's coming to power, he doubted that the

Klingon chief was ignoring him. He had his hands full, no doubt, since seizing the reins after the disastrous civil war that had rent the Empire. In a nation where treachery and assassination were a matter of course, any leader needed to keep his wits about him and his eyes on his back.

The tumultuous days of the Klingon strife came flooding over Picard, and for a moment he felt as though he were once again ensnared in the political machinations of the Klingon Empire.

And once again as though he were confronting the Romulan known as Sela.

This woman had haunted his memories ever since their encounter near the Klingon home world—this apparition, this inexplicable creature. She was the adroit and skillful commander of a Romulan fleet which had attempted to influence the outcome of the Klingon war, and had almost succeeded.

More incredibly, she claimed to be the daughter of Tasha Yar, Picard's chief of security who had died on an away mission some years ago—and who certainly died without ever having had a daughter.

But Sela *looked* exactly like Tasha. Her hair was close-cropped and shaped in the Romulan fashion, but it was the same honey blond as Tasha's, and the jewel-blue eyes were uncomfortably familiar. It was Tasha's face staring at him from the viewscreen, and Tasha's long-limbed body which had paced restlessly around his ready room.

Guinan, who tended the lounge on the *Enterprise* known as Ten-Forward, a woman possessed of mysterious and undeniable metaphysical capacities— capacities which Picard had learned to trust—had insisted that, somehow, Sela was the daughter of Tasha.

Nothing in Picard's experience could explain just who Sela was. But she intruded into his memories nonetheless.

Picard looked up and realized that Worf was staring at him expectantly, wanting to continue the conversation. The captain nodded.

"Gowron," said Worf, "has been rewriting Klingon history." His eyes shone with a particular intensity, which, abetted by the fearsome aspect of his ridged forehead and his towering height, gave him a formidable appearance.

"Rewriting history?" queried Riker.

"He is claiming," said Worf, "that it was his courage—his genius—that brought about an end to the civil war."

"I see."

"In the new version, there is no mention made of the Federation's help in his rise to power." That's why Worf was angry; his captain had been slighted. Picard himself took a more sanguine view. He allowed himself a wry smile.

"It's all right, Mr. Worf. Victors usually rewrite history books. He can take every bit of credit; I'll gladly grant him that. But I need a ship."

Picard considered the situation for a moment, and then said, "If Gowron won't talk to me, get somebody who will, somebody on the High Council, K'Tal perhaps."

"Yes, Captain," said Worf, not happy with this compromise. Picard turned toward Data, who was studying a monitor.

"Captain," he said, "I have a visual identification of

Senator Pardek of Romulus." Picard sat with him and Data activated the monitor.

Picard saw what appeared to be a video log of several Romulans and another alien engaged in what looked like a handshaking session. As they watched, Data explained, "This is a Barolian record of a trade negotiation in which Pardek participated four years ago."

Abruptly, the monitor went blank. "That's all?" queried Picard.

"Yes, sir."

"Run it again."

Data activated the sequence once more, and Picard studied it intently. There was a familiarity to one of the Romulans—had he seen that face before? He tapped a command and it froze on a closeup of the man's face. "Call up the intelligence scan of Spock on Romulus," he directed Data.

And on the screen appeared the shot of Spock that Admiral Brackett had shown him days ago. With him was a Romulan—and Picard realized he was right. "Same man," he stated. "Pardek."

Pardek looked to be in his fifties, but Romulans, like Vulcans, had long life spans and Picard had no guess as to Pardek's true age. If Spock had met him eighty years ago, they were probably nearly the same age—in the fourth decade of their second hundred years.

Pardek was a bit hefty, too—somewhat unusual for a Romulan. He had a round, almost puckish face that gave him a grandfatherly look. He was a bit unique for a Romulan, and Picard was glad for that. He would need to pick Pardek out of a crowd.

"What do we know of him?" he asked.

Picard knew that Data would already have absorbed everything available about Pardek, and Data did not disappoint him, reeling off the information from memory. "He has been in public service since he was a young man, a senator for nine decades. He is considered a 'man of the people,' and has sponsored many reforms. Reportedly, he is considered by the Romulan leadership to be something of a radical because he has been an advocate for peace throughout his career."

"I can see why Spock would cultivate a relationship with him," reflected Picard. "Where are we likely to find him—other than on the floor of the Romulan Senate?"

"The district he represents is called Krocton segment. He maintains a dwelling there."

Picard stared at the image on the monitor. This is the man he would have to find, the man who might lead him to Spock. Pardek of Romulus . . .

"There is more, sir," said Data, breaking into his musing. "I took the liberty of expanding the parameters of my search, and have discovered that Pardek has several relatives in Krocton segment. It is likely that you will be able to locate him there on the third day of the Romulan week, when the Senate is not in session."

Picard smiled at this. "Your resourcefulness never ceases to amaze me, Mr. Data," he said truthfully.

"Thank you, sir."

An idea was forming in Picard's mind. His original thinking had been to go to Romulus alone; one man would cause less suspicion than two, one man was more mobile—and if things went wrong, only one man would be lost.

But a second pair of eyes, a second analytical mind, an unflappable presence for support . . . "If I ever get to Romulus," he said, "I'm going to need help. I'd like you to accompany me."

The android's face reflected both his puzzlement and his pleasure. "Me, sir?"

"Yes."

"I understand how you can be made to look Romulan, sir. But I believe it will be more difficult to transform an android."

"I think Doctor Crusher can come up with something."

"Captain!" Worf's deep voice rang through the bridge. "We are being hailed by the Klingon home world."

Pleased, Picard moved toward him. No cause for alarm, after all, in spite of Worf's anxieties. "Gowron or K'Tal?" he asked.

"Neither, sir." There was the briefest of pauses, and then Worf admitted, "It is the junior adjutant to the diplomatic delegation."

A definite slight. Picard briefly considered his response, then moved toward the viewscreen, asking Worf as he passed, "Name?"

"B'ijik, sir."

"On screen."

B'ijik's outward appearance was traditionally Klingon, though the bony ridge of his skull and forehead was somewhat less pronounced than some, and his long, stringy hair perhaps more tailored. But it was his attitude that leapt off the screen and assaulted Picard. This was a small-minded person, unctuous and officious, who basked in the reflected glory of his superior. He was one of those minions in the ranks of the mighty who have the authority to say "no," but never "yes," and who delight in wielding that small cudgel of power.

"Greetings, Captain," he began breezily. "I am B'ijik, adjutant to Gowron. I regret to inform you that he is quite busy with the High Council and won't be able to speak with you today."

"Is he aware that we've been transmitting messages for three days?"

B'ijik's surprise was clearly feigned. "Messages? I'll have to inspect the logs . . . but I'm sure we haven't received any."

The captain's eyes narrowed. This smarmy little obfuscator was irritating, but Picard kept his voice carefully modulated. "Nonetheless, if you tell Gowron that I have arrived, I'm certain that he will want to talk with me."

B'ijik's smile was simpering and dismissive at once. "Captain, Gowron wishes it were possible to talk with everyone who wants an audience. But he is one man. The demands on his time are formidable. If you would like me to take him a message . . ."

"A message. Very well."

There was a brief moment as Picard stepped forward, working to control the indignation that rose in him at being treated like this by a weaseling functionary. When he spoke, it was a voice that the bridge crew recognized: quiet but foreboding.

"Tell Gowron, Leader of the High Council of the Klingon Empire, that his Arbiter of Succession, Jean-Luc Picard, needs a favor."

"A favor?"

"I require a cloaked vessel."

A faint and condescending smile appeared on B'ijik's lips. "A cloaked vessel. This is no small favor, Captain."

"It is for a mission that could have repercussions throughout the quadrant."

"How would it benefit the Klingon Empire? I'm sure Gowron will ask."

Picard had to take a long moment to control his temper. He longed to give this officious junior officer a tongue-lashing he would remember to his grave, but instead, he said quietly, "The only benefit to the Klingon Empire . . . would be our gratitude."

B'ijik smirked. "That's what you want me to tell Gowron?"

"Yes. And please add that if he is unable to provide a ship, I am sure there are others in the Klingon Empire who would be willing to help me. And then they would have—our gratitude."

That simple statement hung in the air for a moment. Picard knew he had scored, knew that B'ijik was running in his mind the list of Gowron's enemies and had found it formidable. "I see," he replied.

"Also please tell him that I am immensely gratified that he is prospering so well. It is a tribute to his skilled leadership."

B'ijik made no reply to this, merely inclined his head, as though glad to be done with this conversation. His image disappeared and the starfield returned to view. Picard turned around to see Riker had come on the bridge and was listening to this interchange with amusement.

"Nicely done," he offered.

"We'll see." Adrenaline was coursing through Picard's veins—a pleasurable sensation. He enjoyed a challenge and liked getting a bit lathered up now and then. Good for the circulatory system.

Chapter Five

THE SENSATION IN his ear was peculiar: at first a chilling sensation as the interferometric scanner was turned on, and then a slight ringing in his ear—not painful, but somehow unsettling. He was relieved when the process was complete and a three-dimensional model of his ears had been registered in the computer.

He watched as Beverly Crusher turned to inspect Data's ears. The elegantly beautiful doctor, with her porcelain skin and her strawberry red hair, was concentrating fiercely as she peered into the android's ear canal. Data was obediently turning his head this way and that, at Doctor Crusher's request.

They had been in sickbay for half an hour, discussing the necessary prosthetics that would be necessary to transform both him and Data into Romulans. He had every confidence in Beverly; she had accomplished these sophisticated conversions before.

"They aren't removable, are they, Data?" he now heard Beverly ask.

49

"Removable, Doctor?" queried Data, uncertain as to her precise meaning.

"Your ears."

"No, Doctor. They are fully integrated components."

Crusher turned to her assistant. "We'll need molds of his ears, too." The assistant turned to reconfigure the computer, and to scan Data's ears.

"What about his skin color?" Picard asked.

Beverly eyed Data's unique pale skin covering and considered for a moment. "We'll have to do some tests with his pigmentation. Changing it to appear Romulan shouldn't be too hard. I just want to be sure we can change it back again afterwards."

Perhaps he wouldn't mind changing skin color, thought Picard briefly, and then realized that Beverly was coming at him with yet another scanner, which she proceeded to point at his forehead. It was at that moment that he saw Will Riker enter sickbay and stifle a smile at the scrutinizing the captain was undergoing.

"Your right eye," Beverly announced seriously, "is four thousandth higher than the left."

"It is not," retorted Picard, and she grinned at him.

"You want a proper fit on your prosthesis? Trust your tailor."

Picard saw Riker from the corner of his eye, appraising him and the device Beverly continued to move about his face.

"I won't tell a soul about your eyes, sir," Riker said with mock seriousness.

"Anything from Gowron?" asked Picard. The crew had had quite enough fun at his expense. He was becoming eager to get this demeaning procedure over with and get on with his business.

"No, sir. But after your tailor is done, would you join me in the cargo bay? La Forge has made some progress on those metal fragments."

But apparently Doctor Crusher wasn't ready to release her hold on him. "These two still have to report to Mister Mot to get their hairpieces designed," she cautioned. Picard groaned inwardly. The blue-skinned barber would talk his ear off, protracting the process from half an hour to twice that.

Well, he'd have to control the situation. He'd give Mot a half-hour and no more. "Thirty minutes, Number One," he said firmly. Riker nodded and exited.

"Hold still," said Beverly. "I'll never get these measurements right."

The way Mot saw it, a lot of people in Starfleet did a lot of things they just didn't think through too clearly. Take the time they'd delivered Ambassador T'Pel to the Romulans. If they'd asked Mot about that one, he would have told them never to rendezvous with Admiral Mendak. You just had to know that was a questionable move, and sure enough it resulted in handing over a spy with twenty years of classified Starfleet information to reveal to the enemy.

Maybe it was because he had more time to think things out than the average Starfleet officer. His job as ship's barber gave him time to ponder. That's what some of these high-ranking people didn't seem to do. Ponder. Look at things from all sides, turn a situation upside down and backwards and inside out and then back straight on again. Pondering was a unique ability, and one that Mot prided himself on having developed to a fine turn.

That's why it didn't make a lot of sense to him that he wasn't consulted more frequently. He had many times correctly predicted the outcome of one situation or another—usually while the people on the bridge were busy running into themselves or whatever it was they did up there. He was sure he could save everyone a lot of time and trouble if they'd let him get to the heart of the matter and tell them what to do.

Of course, he frequently got the chance to make his views known anyway. The captain came in regularly for a trim, as did commanders Riker and La Forge. You can bet that he didn't miss the opportunity to point out a few of their wrong choices. And they seemed to appreciate it. Eventually, he was sure, they would realize what a prize they had in him and would insist that he not hide his light in the barbershop but join them in important strategy sessions. It was just a matter of time.

Today, he had some very important matters to discuss with the captain. Picard and Commander Data were coming in to get fitted for Romulan hair forms, and Mot intended to show the captain how knowledgeable he was about this current mission. He had no doubt the captain would be amazed.

"Ah, Captain! And Commander Data!" he greeted them as they entered his establishment.

"Mr. Mot, how are you?" asked the captain in his gracious manner. He was a gentleman, no doubt about it.

"Fine, fine," replied Mot. "You gentlemen have a seat and I'll start right in."

"That would be good, Mr. Mot. We're on a rather tight schedule. I have to meet Commander Riker in just half an hour."

"We'll have you out of here in no time," breezed Mot, quickly measuring the captain's skull with an optical scanner. "Let's see . . . I think I've got the basic hair form right here, we'll just see how it fits."

He drew from his supplies a brown hairpiece, which would eventually attach to the scalp with an epidermal adhesive. He placed it in position on the captain's head and inspected it. It was the correct fit, but the hair would have to be trimmed into a Romulan cut; now it was of one length and fell over Picard's eyes, rather like a sheepdog in winter.

"Well, Captain, sounds like you're off on quite an adventure," he began, as he began snipping at the hair form with a laser edge. "Now, mind you, I know it's supposed to be a somewhat secret mission, but of course these things have a way of getting around, and since I'm to make you a Romulan hair form I can certainly put one and one together and get an answer, if you know what I mean."

"Um-hmm," replied the captain, whose eyes were still obscured with hair.

"Of course, I'm not so easily taken in that I think you're actually on your way to Romulus. That would be too obvious, and a man like you would never go in such a straight line. Right?"

"I suppose . . ."

"So, it stands to reason that the Romulan thing is intended to throw everybody off. Make us *think* you're heading for Romulus, so you can get to your real goal while we're misdirected."

"Mmmmm."

"And, all in all, not a bad plan. Everyone looks right—you go left. I like it."

"Thank you."

"Now, maybe you'll use the Romulan getup, maybe you won't. I'm betting you will. You're going under-cover as a Romulan—but *not* to Romulus. So the question becomes, where would you go as a Romulan that wouldn't bring suspicion? And I think I know the answer to that."

"Ah."

Mot snipped and clipped for a moment, drawing out the moment. He knew the captain was wondering if he could possibly have figured out the real plan. And wouldn't he be astonished to find out that Mot—Mot, the barber!—had deduced what was really going on.

"Let's use the process of elimination," Mot contin-ued. "Where might you need to go on a particularly sensitive diplomatic mission? Not a Federation plan-et, that's for sure. And if your real business were with the Klingons, you wouldn't be needing a Romulan disguise. So we're heading for the home world for another purpose—probably for something you need."

There was silence at this. Mot felt that was implied acquiescence. "Romulus, as I've said, is too obvious. Who else does that leave?"

He stopped clipping for a moment as he pondered. It was hard to ponder and trim hair at the same time. One of Picard's eyes looked out from under the Romulan hair; the other was still draped in the brown fringe. Mot looked into the one eye. "The Talarians? I don't think so. No need to go to all this trouble, you'd just go talk to them. The Breen? They're bad ones, all right, but there hasn't been so much as a whisper of any negotiations with them; I don't think we're close to that. The Cateloxes? They've been pretty quiet lately—word is they're having enough trouble with drought on their planet that they're focusing their energies on surviving."

Mot was aware that the captain seemed to be moving a little restlessly in his chair. Awed, no doubt, by this insightful analysis of the Federation's adversaries.

"Now," he continued, "who does that leave? The Murdoth? Too passive. The Phylosians? Vanquished. The Skorr? Irrelevant. The Ferengi? Inconsequential. The Pakleds?"

Picard stirred in the chair. "Forgive me, Mr. Mot, but I really must meet Commander Riker shortly."

"Right, Captain, we'll have you there," said Mot, moving back to his clipping. "Now, where was I? Oh, the Pakleds. Well, I think we'd have to agree there's no problem there." And he threw back his blue head and laughed heartily. The captain smiled.

"So. Where does that leave us?" He tapped the captain's head gently. "I think we both know." Mot leaned in and whispered pointedly. "The Cardassians."

He stood back to assess the captain's response. Picard stared up at him, his second eye now almost uncovered. "The Cardassians," said the captain. His voice gave nothing away—but of course that's what Mot would have expected. Never admit what you know.

"That's right, Captain. I know you didn't think anyone would figure it out—but it's all pretty clear to me. You're going into Cardassian space but you're going as a Romulan. There's an unholy alliance brewing there, I'm willing to bet. So the Cardassians will talk openly with you about their dealings, and you'll get the real story for Starfleet!"

Mot beamed in triumph. Captain Picard gazed up at him with what was clearly admiration. "Mr. Mot," he said, very softly, "I must ask you to keep this information *absolutely* confidential. To do otherwise would jeopardize the security of the mission."

"Me? I wouldn't so much as breathe a word about it. I'm very good at keeping my mouth shut."

"I'm sure of it."

Mot began snipping at the hair form once more. "Now," he continued, "I've had some thoughts about just how to deal with the Cardassians. Seems to me, the mistake that's always made with these people . . ."

He told the captain his entire philosophy about handling the Cardassians, and followed up with a few observations about the potential alliance between Romulus and Cardassia. Picard was impressed, all right, and even if he was a little late for his appointment with Commander Riker, Mot was certain that he was glad for the briefing. It probably wasn't that often that he got the results of such clear and precise thinking.

Riker couldn't have articulated exactly why he was feeling more enthusiastic about this investigation. It was an instinct. When La Forge and his team had finally pieced together the metal fragments and had realized what the object was, its identity was so unexceptional that it would seem likely to have dampened Riker's zeal rather than stimulated it. But that's exactly what made the puzzle alluring to him—the very mundane nature of this piece of equipment.

Now that Captain Picard had finally arrived in the cargo bay—forty-five minutes late—Riker stood with him and Geordi, surveying the hunks of metal arranged on the floor, which had assumed at least partial shape. There were missing sections everywhere, but the chief engineer and his men had done a remarkable job of piecing together this jigsaw. "What we seem to have here, sir," reported Geordi to the captain, "is a navigational deflector array. Or at least what's left of one."

Picard gazed out over the unlikely piece of equipment. "Why would anyone want a Vulcan deflector array?" Riker smiled inwardly. His question exactly.

"Beats me, sir," replied Geordi. Every question we answer here seems to bring up two more."

"You're certain it is Vulcan?"

"Yes, sir. A metallurgical analysis confirmed it, and by running a molecular pattern trace, we even identified the ship as the *T'Pau*. It was decommissioned years ago and sent to the surplus depot at Qualor Two. As far as anyone knows it's still there."

"Worf to Captain Picard." The Klingon's voice boomed throughout the cargo bay. The captain touched his communicator.

"Yes, Lieutenant?"

"A Klingon vessel is decloaking off our port bow. Compliments of Gowron."

Picard and Riker exchanged an amused glance. "Please convey our gratitude, Mr. Worf. Advise the captain that Lieutenant Commander Data and I will be transporting aboard shortly."

"Aye, sir."

So the last obstacle to crossing the Neutral Zone

had been conquered. The captain would soon be on his way. Riker turned to face him.

"If it's all right with you, sir, I'd like to take the *Enterprise* to Qualor Two. See what I can find out there."

The captain didn't take even a moment to consider the request. "By all means, Number One."

Picard extended his hand and Riker shook it. "Good luck, Will."

"And you, sir." Picard nodded and headed for the exit. Riker felt a momentary twinge of regret that he wasn't the one to be embarking on the venturesome journey into the Neutral Zone, but it was quickly replaced with the thought that was to become a refrain for him in the next few days: Who would want a Vulcan deflector array?

Chapter Six

CAPTAIN K'VADA GROWLED as he ate his bowl of *gagh*. It wasn't fresh. A few of the wormlike creatures still stirred, but most were already dead and lay limply in the dish. The best part of eating fresh *gagh* was the sensation of the still-squirming slugs; even after he had bitten through them, they spasmed for several minutes afterward in their death throes, and the unique fluttering continued in his stomach throughout the meal. There was no point to eating them already dead; the taste was dreadful.

He flung the bowl to the side; it bounced and rattled across the bridge of his ship, the Klingon Bird of Prey *Kruge*. Bits of *gagh* splattered onto the deck and the bowl finally rolled under the navigator's console. No one on the bridge reacted with so much as a look; to do so would have been risking severe punishment.

The stale meal was just one more annoyance in a day that was full of them. He had had a terrible fight with his mate, K'kam, and as a result was nursing a painful shoulder. K'kam was strong and agile and possessed of a terrible temper; it was probably a mistake to fight with her. But she made it impossible to avoid. K'Vada growled again as he remembered her obstinate insistence that she leave for an extended tour on a science cruiser bound for the Lambdor system. He was not about to have his mate disappear for such a long time.

He had lost that argument, however, when she dislocated his shoulder. In agony, he agreed to her expedition, and she helped him snap the shoulder back into its socket, but the pain was still intense. And now she would be leaving and he would not have her in his bed again for nearly a year. That is what he would miss; K'kam was as violent in bed as she was in combat, and the experience was incredible.

But by far the worst thing that had happened was his being called by his commanding officer and informed that, by personal order of Gowron, he was to ferry two Starfleet officers to a secret destination. If they failed to return no mention would be made of their deaths; if they came home safely the effort would not be acknowledged. There was no honor in such a mission, and K'Vada resented it deeply.

He had brought his ship alongside the huge starship *Enterprise* and uncloaked, awaiting the transfer of the two officers. He had no idea who they would be; everything about this mission was veiled in secrecy. He didn't like secrets. They made his shoulder ache.

"Two to transport directly to the bridge, Captain," said his first officer. K'Vada nodded and seconds later two men in Starfleet uniforms appeared before him. To his astonishment, one was the captain of the *Enterprise,* Picard, and from the looks of him the other was the android, Data. Whatever mission this was, it was of supreme importance if it required these two senior officers to enter the Neutral Zone.

"Welcome aboard, Captain Picard. I am Captain K'Vada."

"Thank you, sir. This is Lieutenant Commander Data." K'Vada noted that the android was already looking around the bridge, as though assessing its capabilities. He eyed Picard, determined to get some information from him. He assumed his most confronting and challenging tone.

"When I received my orders, Captain, I was not told where we were going." He glared at Picard, demanding an answer.

But none was forthcoming. The distinguished Starfleet officer simply looked at him calmly, making no offer of information. K'Vada pushed on.

"But the heading I was just given takes us into the Neutral Zone—and directly to Romulus."

"That's right." Simple confirmation of the obvious. Nothing more. K'Vada's shoulder throbbed.

"I know my duty, Captain. When I'm given orders, I follow them." He paused and assumed his most intimidating countenance. "But I do not like secrets. They make my shoulder ache." He hoped Picard would think the pain in his shoulder represented a wound received in battle. "I want to know why we are on this mission."

"I'm sorry. It is a confidential matter." Picard seemed not at all intimidated, or even unsettled. His manner was calm, even polite. He was beginning to irritate K'Vada.

"You're going after the defector, aren't you?" K'Vada watched closely to see what impact this statement had. He was sure Picard wouldn't have expected it.

But Picard revealed nothing, his face impassive. "Defector?"

"You think information like that stays a secret? Ambassador Spock has gone to Romulus—and you're going after him." K'Vada stared at Picard, daring him to deny the statement.

But Picard's voice was even as he replied, "Your orders are to take us to a set of coordinates near Romulus, and to bring us back. That is all I am prepared to discuss."

"If we are discovered near Romulus, it means death for all of us."

"I realize that."

K'Vada glowered at Picard, his heavy eyebrows almost meeting in the center from his scowl. But Picard's composure was unshaken. K'Vada realized he would be getting no information from this man. He turned to his helmsman and snapped an order for him to set a course. Then he turned back. "Very well, Captain. We are on our way to Romulus."

"Thank you, Captain. And I do hope your shoulder gets better." K'Vada looked for a hint of sarcasm, but there was none.

Picard had realized within minutes of beaming onto the Klingon ship that Captain K'Vada was spoiling for a fight. He saw nothing to be gained, however, by giving him one. K'Vada looked to him like one whose days of warrior glory were probably behind him, and he had no doubt that the captain of the *Kruge* was rankling under the menial task of providing transportation for Starfleet personnel. He resolved to resist the impulse to rise to argument with the burly Klingon.

When K'Vada flung open the door to the quarters provided for him, however, Picard realized it might be hard to keep that resolve. Judging from the size of the room, K'Vada must have converted a storage closet into a bedroom. It was small, cramped, and bleak. A desk and two chairs were the only furnishings —that and a shelf recessed in the wall, which presumably served as a bed. It had a dank, unused odor, and Picard guessed it hadn't been occupied in a long time.

"Here it is," intoned K'Vada. Then, with thinly veiled sarcasm, "It may not be what you're used to on a Starfleet ship."

Picard took a breath and turned to K'Vada with an even smile. "Quite nice. Thank you." He could see that K'Vada was disappointed in his response, which told him he was correct in adopting this mien.

Data had been inspecting the room with android calm. "Is this the captain's quarters, or mine?"

"Both." Picard couldn't contain a surprised reaction at this. The room was cramped for one person; that two would share it was ludicrous. He saw a spark of victory in K'Vada's eye. "We have limited space. We're a military ship, not a pleasure craft."

"Of course. This will be fine."

Picard noted that K'Vada was feeling better now that he'd scored a hit. The Klingon circled the room, enjoying their momentary discomfiture, pointing out the features. He smacked his hand on the shelf-bed, which bore no mattress, no pillow, no piece of bedding.

"You'll sleep Klingon style. We don't soften our bodies by putting down a pad."

Picard walked to the shelf and smacked it with gusto. "Good. I prefer it that way."

K'Vada eyed him challengingly. "You'll take your meals with us. And we don't serve Federation food."

"I haven't had *gagh* in a long while. I've been looking forward to it. Fresh, if you have it."

K'Vada refused to look at him. "I regret to say, Captain, that my *patahk* of a cook has not stored the freshest of *gagh*. I hope you would not be displeased to have it as I myself eat it."

Picard inclined his head politely. "It would be an honor." Picard sensed that K'Vada was listening carefully for the sound of any revelatory emotion— dismay or disgust—and he was careful to keep his voice neutral.

K'Vada turned to survey the room once more, then started toward the door. He hesitated, and Picard wondered uneasily what this gruff, threatened man had in store now. When K'Vada turned back to them, there was what passed for a smile on his face.

"One more thing. Our passage into the Neutral Zone is illegal and hence dangerous. I will require all nonessential personnel to remain in their quarters at all times."

Picard felt astonishment rising in him and fought it back. *Stay in these miserable quarters?* He tried to keep his features composed, but from the flash of satisfaction in K'Vada's face he knew he had not completely succeeded. "Surely you can't mean the two of us, Captain. We are Starfleet personnel. We are accustomed to the dangers of combat."

But K'Vada knew he had scored a touch, and he would not yield that slight advantage. "As captain, I am responsible for all persons on my ship. For your own safety I must require you to stay confined." He smiled, showing small, stained teeth in which bits of his lunch were still imbedded, and withdrew.

Picard turned to see Data's imperturbable face regarding him calmly. "It would seem, sir, that we are to see a great deal of one another. May I suggest that an amusing way of passing the time would be to play a game? It involves arranging higher polynomials into sets of rational coefficients. I have found it so absorbing at times that the hours seem to pass like minutes."

Picard let out a sigh. He walked to one of the chairs in the room—an ill-formed piece of furniture with no cushioning—tugged at his jacket, and sat down. "By all means, Mr. Data. That sounds captivating."

Chapter Seven

SEEN UP CLOSE in the subdued lighting of Ten-Forward, Gretchen Naylor's eyes were even more remarkable than they had seemed before. A pale green, almost translucent, framed by heavy, dark lashes, they were almost otherworldly. But Naylor was human, born and raised on Earth, in the North American agricultural paradise of Indiana. Riker had visited Indiana once as a schoolboy, and had been struck with the rural beauty of the rolling hills and verdant plains. With the advent of sophisticated replicator technology the need for vast acres of corn and soybeans had been obviated; land in the state had been converted to huge agricultural parks devoted to the production of flowers, herbs, and medicinal plants. A patchwork of color extended as far as the eye could see— burgundies, corals, silver greens—and the air was sweet with heady fragrances.

Perhaps it was living in such an Eden that produced people of such bountiful friendliness and generosity. Riker could still remember the warmth and affection

of the family he stayed with, the immediate acceptance with which he was welcomed, and the friendships he maintained for many years. The people of his
native Alaska were decent and honest, to be sure, and
above all hardworking; but more of their energies had
to be devoted to simple survival, leaving less time to
the nurturing of friendships. He wasn't sure he would
have traded his childhood in Alaska, for it gave him
disciplines and strengths for which he was grateful.
But his visit to the balmy, fragrant hills of Indiana
would stay with him all his life.

Gretchen Naylor was typical of Indiana natives in
her straightforward honesty, but she didn't have the
easygoing, relaxed quality that he remembered from
his youth. There was a drive to this woman, an
underlying eagerness to achieve. That would have
been a necessity, of course, for her admittance to
Starfleet Academy. One did not beat out the twelve
thousand applicants for each position by hanging
back.

". . . and then I was posted to the *Reliant.* I served
there for two years as junior security officer. When a
position opened on the *Enterprise* I couldn't believe it.
Everyone wants to be here. When I applied I didn't
really think there was a chance. But I got it—and my
friends said they could hear me whooping all over the
ship." She smiled, a wide, bounteous smile that
illuminated her face. She bent to sip her fruit drink,
and little wisps of her dark hair fell forward over her
face. Just as Riker had imagined.

"I'm sure it's our good fortune to have you here,
Ensign." Riker was being careful to preserve the
formality of the relationship. Naylor had been
assigned—by Worf—to provide research and intelli-

gence on the Zakdorn, the race who operated the surplus depot at Qualor Two. Riker had been secretly pleased with her choice, and the selection of Ten-Forward as a location for the briefing had been his; but he was still wary of the dangers of shipboard romance, and this green-eyed woman stirred him too deeply to ignore those risks.

"Would you like to hear what I've learned about the Zakdorn, sir?" She had picked up on the businesslike tone of his voice and was responding in kind. Bright woman. If they could have met in other circumstances . . .

"By all means." He settled back as she placed a padd on the table and began keying instructions.

"The Zakdorn are one of the more recent species to be admitted to the Federation. They are a peaceful race with no real enemies. They achieved warp-drive capacity relatively early in their development because all their resources could be channeled toward scientific development." *Unlike Earth,* Riker thought. He nodded for her to continue.

"Their strengths seem to lie in their penchant for organization and efficiency. They lack a creative imagination and have almost no native art forms. They are superior accountants, bookkeepers, and mapmakers."

Riker grinned. "They sound like a dull lot. A planet of bureaucrats." She smiled back, nodding. "My thoughts exactly. But perfect for receiving and storing out-of-use space ships."

"I guess that's why they have the largest of the surplus shipyards." There were three other depots that the Federation maintained in various sectors, but the one at Qualor Two had swollen mightily in the last twenty years. Several thousand ships, in varying states of repair, had found a resting place there, ranging from proud vessels rendered inoperable in battle to ships that had simply become outmoded as new designs took their place. Riker had never visited one of these graveyards, and he was curious to see it.

But most of all, he was curious to see the *T'Pau*, to find if the Vulcan ship offered any clues as to how its deflector array could have wound up in the hands of the Ferengi.

He pushed back his chair. "Good work, Ensign. We should be in orbit of Qualor Two by tomorrow at eleven hundred hours. This information will be put to good use."

Naylor nodded and pushed her chair back, collected her padd, and stood.

"I'll be happy to escort you to your quarters," offered Riker.

"Thank you, sir, it's not necessary," she said, to his disappointment. Then she paused and gazed at him with those strange pale eyes. They seemed to spark and flash as they reflected light from the room. "I'm happy you're pleased with my work, Commander. Please don't hesitate to ask for anything more you might need."

Suddenly Riker felt himself as insecure as a schoolboy with a crush. Was there a double entendre in her statement? Or was he projecting his own feelings, reading something he wanted to be there? That there was something needy emanating from Gretchen Naylor he didn't doubt. Just what it was, he couldn't define.

"Thank you, Ensign," he said formally, and she

turned and walked toward the door. Riker watched, trying not to be affected by the sight of her willowy form swaying in front of him.

"Most Romulans live in multi-unit structures known as 'takas.' There are few single-unit dwellings, and they are reserved for those in power. Population density in the capital city is forty thousand per square kilometer." Picard stretched his neck as he read from the information on the padd; they'd been at it for hours and he felt the stiffness throughout his body from having sat so long in the Klingon chair, which he had by now decided was a cleverly planned torture device.

"Pardek's neighborhood, Krocton segment," added Data, "is in one of the older parts of the city." He didn't read from a padd; he had undoubtedly absorbed every particle of intelligence contained in it some time ago and was now reciting from memory. "It is a lower-class area of no architectural distinction. He has maintained a taka there for many years."

"Krocton segment," murmured Picard. "That's where we'll plan to transport." He looked up at Data and realized he was very glad indeed that he had brought this valued officer with him. The journey might have been even more of an ordeal if he had chosen to undertake it alone. Data's calm and steady presence was reassuring; and certainly this cram-session study of the Romulans was more pleasurable with the two of them.

Picard rolled his neck again, working out the kinks. He felt genuinely weary, and realized it must be well past the time he usually retired.

"That's enough for me, Data," he said. "I think I'll turn in."

Data cast his eyes about the barren room. "Since I do not require sleep, I propose you take the—" The android hesitated, not sure what to call the dismal hole in the wall that was to pass for a bed. "—the shelf. I will be content to stand."

"Very well, Mr. Data. Thank you." Picard headed toward the shelf, eyeing it warily. It was about four feet off the deck—an awkward position for entering —and only about two feet in height. Getting into the damned thing would require an act of contortion. Picard felt ungainly and clumsy as he climbed in, cracking his head and both his shins during the process.

Once he was settled, he found himself lying on a bare board surface, staring up at the underside of the shelf barely more than a foot away. He rolled his head to the side and saw Data staring at him imperturbably. "Are you comfortable, sir?" he asked.

"I suppose so," replied Picard evenly.

"Then good night, Captain. Sleep well."

"Thank you."

Picard closed his eyes, determined to relax and get the sleep he knew he needed. He'd slept in uncomfortable places before, after all; it was merely a matter of concentrating, of blocking outside annoyances and allowing the mind to drift aimlessly . . . perhaps enhanced by a bit of fantasy . . . a restful lagoon, a tropical breeze, exotic trees bending in the warm winds . . . waves lapping on a shore . . .

His eyes snapped open and he turned toward Data. "What are you doing?"

Data looked puzzled and concerned. "Sir? Was I making noise?"

"Not exactly."

"I was processing information we have accumulated on Romulan society. I am preparing for the task of impersonating a Romulan."

"I see."

"Would you like me to discontinue?"

"No, no. Please go ahead." Picard was annoyed with himself. Of course he couldn't hear Data processing information; it was a silent function, just like thought. It was just that he *knew* Data was doing it. He could almost see the circuitry in Data's head, blinking and twinkling as millions of bits of information sped along his neutral nets. Of course, maybe it *did* make a sound, no matter how slight, and that could explain why Picard found it difficult to relax, knowing that all those remarkable functions were occurring in the positronic brain of someone not four feet from him—

His eyes opened again and he almost gasped as he saw Data staring at him. "What are you looking at?"

Again, Data was puzzled. "I am not looking at anything, sir. I am continuing to organize my files."

"But you're looking at me."

"I am sorry if I am disturbing you, sir. I will not look in your direction." And he swiveled so that the back of his head was toward Picard. The captain eyed him for a moment, feeling sheepish and annoyed at the same time. He realized it had been many years since he had had what might qualify as a roommate, and even then, at Starfleet Academy, it was not an arrangement he particularly savored.

"Mr. Data . . ."

"Yes, sir?"

"Could you possibly—sleep?"

"I do not think so, sir."

"I see." Picard closed his eyes once more. He was not going to be defeated. He was a man used to taking charge of his circumstances; quieting the mind required only certain techniques of relaxation and focus . . . relaxation . . . focus . . .

Relaxation . . . focus . . .

Relaxation . . .

Picard crawled out from the confining space. Data looked at him with quizzical eyes.

"Sir? Do you not wish to sleep?"

"I don't think so. Shall we continue to go over the files?"

"I would be happy to." Without further ado, Data began rattling off facts. "I have been studying Krocton segment, as you asked, and have selected several appropriate sites for our transport. I will describe each of them to you."

Picard stifled a yawn and sat once more in the chair of pain.

By 0900 hours the next morning, the *Enterprise* was within hailing range of Qualor Two, and Riker instructed Worf to make contact. He was too impatient to wait until they achieved orbit. It seemed to take forever for Worf to establish the connection, but finally the Klingon announced from his tactical station that he had been successful.

"On screen," Riker ordered, rising and stepping forward, eager to speak to the Zakdorn who might unlock some of the mysteries of his mission.

The humanoid who appeared before him was not at all what Riker expected. He was grizzled and worn, a graying hulk who had perhaps taken on the aspect of the abandoned ships he oversaw. He looked vaguely surprised, as though he had been interrupted in the middle of something. A small frown knotted his brow; the characteristic Zakdorn folds in the skin of his face seemed draped in remonstration.

"I'm Commander William Riker of the Federation starship *Enterprise*," said Riker, in an amiable fashion.

"Klim Dokachin here, quartermaster of Surplus Depot Zed-one-five." The man's tone was terse, uninviting, offering nothing more than a statement of fact.

"We need some information about a Vulcan ship, the *T'Pau*," continued Riker. "It was sent there a few years ago."

"Did you arrange an appointment?"

Riker was sure he looked as startled as he felt. The question was completely unexpected.

"Appointment? No . . ."

"Then I can't help you. Communicate with Scheduling."

And with that the transmission was abruptly ended and Riker found himself staring at a starfield. He was nonplussed. He turned to Counselor Deanna Troi for vindication. "Who does this guy think he is?"

But Troi's dark eyes sparkled as she replied calmly, "The quartermaster of the surplus yard, Commander. With information you need."

Riker absorbed that for a moment. It was Troi's way of communicating that he would need to use a different tactic if he wanted to get information from this recalcitrant old bureaucrat. He drew a breath. "Right. Mr. Worf, reestablish communication."

"Yes, sir."

A moment later Dokachin appeared on the screen once more, somewhat taken aback at having been interrupted again. Riker gave him a friendly smile. "Mr. Dokachin—"

That was as far as he got before the man interrupted. *"Ah*chin. Klim Dok*ah*chin."

Riker took a breath. "Mr. Dok*ah*chin, the information I need involves a matter of major importance to the Federation."

"Yes?" Dokachin looked unimpressed.

"I'll need access to your logs, your files . . ." he trailed off, but Dokachin made no reply. He plunged ahead gamely. "It won't take long . . . my people can do the work."

There was a lengthy pause. Dokachin stroked his chin, drummed his fingers, and looked at the ceiling. Finally, he announced, "I don't let outsiders into my computer system."

"Fine. One of your people, then . . ." Riker would have agreed to anything to overcome this annoying obstacle.

"Wish I had the people to spare. I don't."

Riker made himself stay calm, but he could feel his heart starting to punch a little harder. There was an edge to his voice as he asked, "Well, sir—what would you suggest?"

"I don't know. Contact me when you reach orbit."

And the starfield returned. Riker turned again to Troi, pulsing with indignation. "I don't believe him." But Troi's beautiful mouth curled into a wry smile.

"He's king of his particular hill, Commander. You'll have to treat him that way."

Riker stared at her, and didn't miss a beat as he replied, "Counselor—a perfect job for you."

And he sat. One of the requisites of command was the ability to delegate responsibility. This was one case in which he was only too glad to do so.

Counselor Deanna Troi stifled the smile that sprang to her lips when Will Riker passed the responsibility of dealing with Klim Dokachin to her. She wasn't surprised, and she really couldn't blame him—the man was irritating, no question. And he was the kind that an impatient man like Will would have a lot of trouble tolerating.

Troi didn't mind being assigned the handling of Dokachin; it fell well within the boundaries of her responsibilities on board the *Enterprise.* One reason she enjoyed her post was the opportunity to rise to the unique challenges involved in dealing with alien personalities.

But the more races she encountered, the more she was aware of the constants. There were far more similarities than dissimilarities in the psyches of the multitudes of species she had experienced. Most responded to nurturing, kindness, compassion, and understanding. Most disliked assault, rudeness, insensitivity, and humiliation. This meant that it was usually wise for her to follow her own empathic instincts when meeting a new race.

She frankly thought dealing with Klim Dokachin would be like melting butter. He seemed transparent to her in his need for ego stroking. He was a being whose identity was deeply involved with his work, who derived his satisfaction from the execution of his duties, and who wanted to be recognized for his expertise. It would not be difficult to give him what he needed.

Gazing out at the starfield as they raced toward Qualor Two, Troi felt a momentary twinge of melancholy. She had been in some turmoil lately, examining her life and trying to come to some decisions about her priorities. She did not particularly enjoy this process; by nature she was given to equanimity, and tended to accept life as it was dealt to her without a great deal of angst or examination.

But something extraordinary had happened to her recently, and she felt irreparably changed by it. The whole experience had taken less than twenty hours, and yet she knew that it had altered her life.

It had been a strange set of circumstances that had led to the situation. She was on the bridge with Chief O'Brien when Will Riker was busy elsewhere and the captain had taken three young winners of the school science fair on a tour. A chance phenomenon, the collision with a quantum filament, had catastrophically damaged the *Enterprise* and killed the bridge duty officer, Lieutenant Monroe.

Sealed off from the rest of the ship, with communications systems down, Troi found herself the ranking officer on the bridge—and as such, acting captain.

It had been frightening at first; she wasn't familiar with emergency protocols and if it hadn't been for O'Brien and Ensign Ro she would have floundered.

But the situation called for her to make a difficult and risky command decision, one in which she had to reject the intelligent option for which Ro argued eloquently. She had stood everyone down, trusting her own instincts—and won the day.

A horrible phrase came to mind, one she knew was used in reference to Terran animals: *the taste of blood.* It was said that a newborn wild animal who had lost its mother might be tamed if it were retrieved shortly after birth. But if it were allowed the taste of blood—a fresh kill—its feral nature would be stirred, and the animal would revert to its primitive state, never again satisfied with the tepid pleasures of domesticity.

The phrase had been running through Troi's head ever since she had risen to the moment and captained the ship in a time of crisis. Since then, nothing had come close to providing the heady excitement of that experience. She performed her tasks competently, and she was sure no one was aware of her inner confusion. But the world of the *Enterprise* seemed to her drawn in tones of sepia—colorless and pale. She felt an indescribable yearning for something wild and potent in her life, something extraordinary.

Her mother, she knew, would tap into those feelings instantly if she were on board. But her solution was not one that would satisfy Troi. Lwaxana was still entreating her to abandon this demanding career, return to Betazed, get married, and have children. Troi believed that someday she would probably do just that—but she wasn't anywhere near ready. Lwaxana's pleas had far more to do with her desire to become a grandmother than with Deanna's desire for home and hearth.

"We are approaching the orbital surplus yard of Qualor Two," announced Worf, and Troi noted that she was comforted by the gruff, sure tones of the Klingon. She gazed at the viewscreen and saw that they were coming on an incredible sight: a vast ocean of spaceships—old, abandoned, decommissioned—stretching as far as the sensors could see, a graveyard of once proud ships from throughout the Federation. It was an eerie sight, this silent armada of ghostly vessels, and she realized with a sudden shiver that each of those abandoned hulks represented stories of ordeal, daring, and mystery. She thrilled for a moment to imagine the incredible events that had befallen them. And wondered if ever again she would taste the raw excitement of untrammeled adventure.

Deanna honestly didn't know just what it was she was seeking. She was sure, however, that if it presented itself, she would recognize it.

Riding the turbolift from the *Enterprise* transporter room, Klim Dokachin fought dizziness. Transporter technology had been introduced to his planet when they became members of the Federation, and he had not adapted well to it. He'd thought of holding firm in his insistence that the officers of the starship *Enterprise* come to *him* if they wanted his records so badly; but in the end he couldn't resist the opportunity to see what the magnificent vessel looked like. When the turbolift door opened and he stepped onto the bridge, he was glad he'd done so.

He felt the eyes of the bridge crew as he took his time gazing around, and he was glad he had on his best outfit—one that held the emblems of merit he had achieved through his work. They would realize this was no raw novice they were dealing with.

As he inspected the bridge of the vast starship, he could sense the anxiousness of the crew. The tall one with the beard, with whom he'd spoken on the communicator, was particularly impatient. Well, he could wait. Klim Dokachin was doing this on *his* terms, and he wasn't about to be hurried.

"Thank you for coming on board, Mr. Dokachin."

That from the bearded one. He was trying to win him over; Klim could hear it in his voice. Well, maybe he'd be won over, maybe not. He'd take his time before he decided how he felt about that one.

He strolled down the ramp and inspected Ops and Conn. Everything was immaculate, shining, functional. Dokachin thought it was perhaps the most beautiful ship he'd ever seen.

"Not bad," he said dryly.

The beard was following him around the bridge, trying to get his attention. "We've tied into your computers. If you could access the files . . ."

Dokachin continued his slow tour, inspecting the consoles and the forward turbolift. "I don't usually see them in such good condition. By the time they get to me, they're falling apart."

From the corner of his eye, Dokachin could see the beard turn and look at someone—a woman in a form-fitting gray jumpsuit. She began to move toward him and Klim turned to meet her.

She was the most beautiful creature he had ever seen.

He had never found humans particularly attractive —the way their skin was so tightly drawn over the bones of their faces looked positively painful—and this woman looked human. Though there was something different about her eyes—they were the darkest black imaginable. Her hair was black, too, but her skin was pale and delicate. Too taut, but delicate.

"Mr. Dokachin, we must find this ship—and you're the only one who can help us." Her voice was gentle, and her eyes were friendly as she smiled at him. And Klim Dokachin realized that what made her beautiful was not the way she looked, but what was within. There was a beautiful soul within this woman, and it shone from her like a radiant moonrise.

"Who are you?" he asked.

"Deanna Troi, ship's counselor."

Dokachin moved closer to her, nodded his head toward Riker. "He probably figures we don't get to see women like you very often. And you might get more cooperation from me." He smirked inwardly that he was one step ahead of the beard.

Then he looked into those black eyes again. "He's probably right," he said, and found himself moving to one of the consoles at the aft portion of the bridge, the beautiful woman following. The beard trailed along. Klim began expertly keying instructions into the computer, hoping that the woman would realize how proficient he was at his task.

"The *T'Pau*, wasn't it? Vulcan registry . . ." He gestured as the information instantly leapt to the screen. "There. Logged in on Stardate 41334."

"Where is the ship now?" Klim looked up at the sound of a different voice. This might be a nonhuman, he wasn't sure. The skin was dark and the being wore a device around his eyes.

"Docked," Klim replied. "Section eighteen-gamma-twelve. Want me to take you over there?"

"I'd appreciate that," the beard said.

"Helmsman," said Dokachin with a touch of command in his voice, "lay in a heading one-four-one by two-zero-eight. Ahead slow, two hundred kph." They'd realize he knew his way around ships before he was done. Knew his way around before most of them had been born, probably.

He noted that the helmsman didn't act on the command until the beard had nodded to him. That was irritating for an instant, until the beautiful woman fastened those melting black eyes on him and said, in her haunting voice, "It must be so difficult to keep track of all these ships. How ever do you do it?"

Dokachin smiled at her. He'd pegged her right away as a woman of intelligent curiosity. She would appreciate the near genius of his classification procedure, with its dozens of systems and subsystems. His peers found it so complex and intricate that they had trouble following it, but Klim was sure that this woman would not only grasp it but value its elaborate mysteries.

"Well," he said, settling himself next to her, "the first problem is the initial gross assessment. Now, you may think that's a simple task, but that's where people get into trouble right at the start."

The woman nodded, and Klim knew he had her riveted.

Riker gazed at the viewscreen as they navigated their way toward the *T'Pau.* They moved at a cautious pace through the immense graveyard of ships, skirting their way carefully through the ghostly flotsam. Occasionally Riker would recognize a name or a design; once Worf announced that they were passing the *Ghandi,* a legendary ship whose exploits Riker had studied at the Academy, and whose last explorations he had chronicled in a junior thesis. He was stunned to see the ship whose crew he had described in intimate detail, floating immobilized and impotent in space, a burned-out shell that had been the victim of violence while on a nonviolent mission, as though its name had determined its fate. He briefly held his hand over his heart as they passed by, in tribute.

To his rear, he heard the steady, droning tones of Klim Dokachin, describing to Deanna in crushing detail his record-keeping mechanism. Riker briefly tuned in.

". . . and then you have to make subcategories according to tonnage. Some people like to classify by propulsion system, but I find that can lead to confusion. A galaxy-class ship like this one, for instance, employs a fifth-phase reactor. But you might find that in a scout ship, too. It gets messy."

"I can see that," murmured Troi, and Riker smiled to himself. Her eyes must be glazing over by now.

"Commander," interjected Worf's brusque voice, "we are approaching the designated coordinates."

"On screen," said Riker, and everyone turned expectantly to see the Vulcan ship.

What they saw was the starfield—empty space.

Klim Dokachin's jaw dropped when he found himself staring at section eighteen-gamma-twelve and there was no ship in sight. One moment he had held the beautiful woman enraptured with his discourse on the surplus depot, now he was staring at what seemed to be proof that his immaculate record-keeping system was faulty.

He felt the others looking at him, puzzled, as he stepped toward the screen. "Where is it?" he breathed, staring at the starfield as though he could will the Vulcan ship to appear. "What happened to it?" *Check the coordinates,* his mind told him, and he stepped to the console, tapped carefully. Glancing over his shoulder he found the ship had not magically appeared. "These are the correct coordinates," he found himself saying apologetically.

The beard spoke. "The *T'Pau* is missing?"

"The *T'Pau*," began Klim intently—and then he looked up at the starfield, and back at the array of faces looking expectantly at him—"is missing," he intoned.

The beard's eyes narrowed. "How could a ship disappear from your depot?"

Klim began to feel chastened. His professional integrity was being questioned. He drew a deep breath and turned back to the console. He would not crumble before these judgmental intruders.

"I'm not accustomed to losing things, Commander," he said resolutely. "I'll find your ship for you." He began to work the keys with furious intent. "I have the *T'Pau* cross-referenced in four different directories."

"When it was brought here, was it stripped of materiel—armament, sensors?" This was from the dark one with the instrument on his eyes.

"Of course," said Dokachin, still working to locate the missing ship.

"Can you tell us what happened to its navigational deflector?"

Klim looked at the monitor. He had accessed a processing file on the *T'Pau* and was able to determine the disposition of its materiel. "It was routed to the *Tripoli,* a holding vessel on the outer rim of the shipyard."

The beard jumped in. "It's not there anymore.

What's left of that deflector is laid out on the floor of our cargo bay."

Suddenly Klim Dokachin was frightened. Things beyond his control were happening. He had trusted his records, his books, his files, and they were crumbling before him. Until now, if his computer said something was stored somewhere, that's where it was. There was surety in his system. If that was gone, what else was there? How could he count on anything?

"How can that be?" he breathed weakly.

"Maybe we ought to pay a visit to the *Tripoli,*" said the beard. Dokachin realized he was afraid to go there.

But of course they did. He gave the coordinates to the helmsman—he tried to make his voice sound as confident as the first time—and they maneuvered their way through the shipyard. Dokachin was silent for a long time, his mind racing to find a rational explanation for the missing ship. But none of the possibilities he constructed held up for very long. It would seem he had made an error. The *T'Pau* was not in space eighteen-gamma-twelve; it was somewhere else, and he couldn't imagine how to begin tracking it. Had someone made a logging error? Had some junior computer operator assigned the ship to another space and failed to make the correct entry?

But he himself always checked those entries, just to prevent something like this from happening. He felt himself sinking lower into the chair, the weight of his misery crushing him.

"Mr. Dokachin, I'm sure there's a reason for this, and we'll find it." It was the beautiful woman with her beautiful voice and her beautiful sensitivity. He took refuge in the comfort of her large, dark eyes; it was as though he dared not look away from them. For the first time, he felt like speaking.

"In all the time the Zakdorn have operated this depot, nothing's ever been lost," he assured her. *"Never."* She nodded sympathetically and he felt better. "I'll tell you this—somebody will pay. I'll conduct an investigation. Whoever is responsible—"

"Approaching the coordinates of the *Tripoli,* sir." The guttural growl of a formidable Klingon interrupted Dokachin's discourse. Klim felt himself go queasy, and he was aware that the beard looked in his direction.

He tried to appear nonchalant.

"On screen," said the beard.

The *Tripoli* was not in its assigned docking position. Dokachin was devastated. "I do not understand this. This is not possible." His universe was giving way beneath him. Nothing made sense.

"We beam goods to the *Tripoli* on a regular schedule," said Dokachin desperately. "There was a shipment yesterday, and another is set for today. It *must* be there."

"When is today's transport?"

"Just over two hours from now. A shipment of deuterium storage tanks."

The beard considered this for a moment, then turned toward the Conn. "Ensign, align the *Enterprise* so we'll appear to be one of the abandoned ships. Mr. La Forge, when we're in position, shut down engines and all systems except sensors and life support."

"Aye, sir."

The beard moved toward a chair that Dokachin assumed was that of command.

"I'm guessing somebody's going to be here to receive those sensors—and I'd be very interested to see who it is."

Hearing the man's quiet authority, Dokachin felt better. He looked at the woman, and she smiled warmly at him. For the first time, he felt a camaraderie with these starship people. Whatever was going on here, they were in it together.

Chapter Eight

THIS TIME Picard knew it was a dream and he struggled to come out of it. He was flailing in a cloud of cold fog, crying and raging; another man was standing a distance away, struggling to free him from the oppressive cloud. Or perhaps that second person was himself . . . a second Picard . . . ? Who was it? He strained to make his way toward the man, but the roiling billows of icy vapor took on substance, and kept him from moving forward.

He could not remember ever being so cold. It was a bitter, damp cold that seeped into his muscles and joints and paralyzed them with pain. And it was such a sad thing to be cold; he sobbed with grief. Then, still wracked with anguish, he felt anger rising, a fury at the cold and damp, a frenzied flame within him, which ripped through his insides until he became uncontrollably furious. He raged at the crippling chill, shrieking his wrath until the sheer force of his fury helped warm him.

No! This weakness disgusts me! I hate it! Where is the logic? I am betrayed . . . betrayed . . . betrayed . . .

Someone else was with him now—was it the figure he had seen before? And who was he?—trying to pull him from the icy bog. A pinpoint of light appeared in the depths of the foggy mists, a light that glowed golden, spreading larger and larger, casting a warmth that seemed to melt the numbing cold, an orb that grew bigger and brighter, heat, welcome heat . . .

Where had the other man gone?

Picard opened his eyes and found himself looking into Data's face, his yellow eyes reflecting concern. "Sir? Perhaps we have studied sufficiently. You might want to go to bed."

Picard sat upright in the chair and discovered himself still in the cramped quarters on the Klingon ship *Kruge*. He felt as though he had been out for hours. "How long was I asleep, Mister Data?" he asked, his mouth dry and his voice hoarse.

"I do not believe you were asleep, sir," replied the android. "You closed your eyes for only a fraction of a second."

Picard stared at him briefly, then dropped his eyes to the padds on the table. They had been studying Romulan culture. It seemed like hours ago. He picked up his padd and keyed it, wanting desperately to regain a feeling of normalcy. He forced himself to focus on the padd, where the words blurred and swam before his eyes. He squeezed his eyes shut until he felt sure that when he opened them, they would behave as he willed.

Sarek was part of him. Whenever he slept, Sarek crept inside him, possessing him, becoming him. As he drew nearer to Spock, he could feel Sarek more and more strongly.

Picard was startled when the door opened suddenly and K'Vada strode in. The strapping Klingon captain looked as threatening as ever and yet Picard sensed not menace but something he couldn't quite pinpoint. A certain solicitude? Puzzled, Picard gazed up at him.

"Captain. In monitoring subspace messages we picked up a piece of information that might interest you." He handed a padd to Picard, who glanced at it, instantly absorbed the message, and had to steel himself to respond in a normal voice.

"Thank you, Captain." K'Vada gazed at him for a moment more, as though something might be forth-coming, then nodded and withdrew.

Data was staring at him, waiting patiently for an explanation to this peculiar scene. Picard turned to him and, as evenly as he could, read the message.

"Sarek is dead."

He heard himself say the words and that gave them reality; until that moment he wasn't sure if he might not be back in the dream. But the close Klingon quarters were real, and the dim lighting, and the miserable chair, and Data gazing at him with imper-turbable saffron eyes. And the padd in his hand was real, and so, he knew, was its message.

He turned to the chair and sat, feeling disoriented. The room spun slightly and he fastened his eyes on the padd.

Then he felt something icy move through him, and he shivered.

Riker felt like laughing. Or humming. Or pacing or driving his fist into his palm. Instead, he sat in the command chair, staring at the viewscreen as though at any moment it would provide the answer to the question they were all asking: Who was receiving the transport of the materiel routinely beamed to a cargo ship that apparently no longer existed?

Riker could feel his heart rate rising; the hammer of his pulse in his temple sounded like timpani. It was a heady, sensual feeling and he reveled in it. It brought to bear sensations with which he was not consciously in touch—the thrill of hunt, of combat, and conquest, akin to lust. Was it racial memory? There was certainly nothing in his experience that would account for the feelings coursing through him now as they waited silently in the black cold of space for a confrontation with the unknown.

But he no longer felt restless.

He stared at the viewing screen, which showed only an inky space punctuated by stars. His eyes burned into the image, seeking anything abnormal, when—

"Commander, sensors detect a ship approaching at warp speed." Worf's announcement was a crisp growl.

The pulse in Riker's temple drummed harder.

"Identification?"

"Negative. No transponder signal. No subspace marker."

"Sounds like they don't *want* to be identified." This a staccato punctuation from Geordi.

"The ship is coming out of warp now," continued Worf.

Riker stared at the viewscreen, scrutinizing it with fierce concentration, looking for the covert ship. He could see a faint blip, almost indistinguishable.

"Magnify," he breathed, and the blip jumped into relief.

It was dark, huge, and ominous. It was bristling with armament but carried absolutely no marking of any kind. Riker stared at it, breathless, awed by its proud malevolence.

"Sensors indicate a combat vessel . . . origin undetermined . . . heavily armed." Geordi's composed voice seemed at odds with the fearsome image he described. "Mass and density suggest it's fully loaded with cargo. From the look of these internal scans, I'd guess a good part of that cargo is weaponry."

Riker watched as the dark ship swung away from them and slowed. "The ship is moving into section twelve-beta-three," announced Worf.

"It's taking the position assigned to the *Tripoli,*" said the Zakdorn. "The coordinates are identical."

"Commander," interrupted Geordi, "readings indicate the surface-to-ship transport has begun."

This produced an instant and irate reaction from Dokachin. "He's taking *my* deuterium tanks!"

"Bring the engines back on line, Mr. La Forge," said Riker, "and restore all systems to normal."

But the sinister ship wasn't waiting around now that it had the goods. "He's powering up engines, sir," barked Worf.

"Open a channel," retorted Riker, and rose to approach the screen.

"Open, sir."

"This is Commander William Riker of the U.S.S. *Enterprise.* Identify yourself."

Several seconds passed, in the silence of which Riker could feel his heart pelting his rib cage. "I repeat: you have entered a Federation depot. Identify yourself."

"Sir, the ship is locking phaser banks."

"Shields up. Red alert."

The whine of red alert and the red flashing strobes signaled the onset of combat readiness. Riker could feel the tension on the bridge rise another notch. "That ship easily matches our armament, Commander," Geordi noted.

That was a theory Riker hoped he didn't have to prove. On the screen, they all watched as the giant ship slowly hove to and swung to face them. Riker stepped a bit closer to the screen.

"If you do not respond to our hails, we will take that as evidence of hostile action."

"There is an energy buildup in their phaser banks—sir, they are activating weapons!" roared Worf, and before Riker could respond, a mighty WHUMP! struck the *Enterprise,* jolting them and causing lights to flicker. Worf's voice cut through the commotion. "Forward shields down to seventy-two percent—"

"Boost power to the shields," snapped Riker. "Mr. Worf, target their weapon systems only and prepare to fire—" But the other ship had already loosed another barrage and the *Enterprise* took an even heavier wallop. Several of the bridge consoles sparked furiously, and emergency lighting sprang on.

"Forward shields at sixty-eight percent, aft shields forty percent."

"On my mark, a point-seven-five burst only. We just want to slow them down." Geordi might feel that the dark ship was their match, but Riker felt sure the *Enterprise* weapons could fatally damage the other vessel, and he wanted to avoid that. He was more interested in answers than in destruction.

"Mr. Worf—fire," he ordered curtly, and Worf let

loose with a staggered phaser array. Riker knew it wouldn't cause irreparable harm to such a sturdy ship, but it would sure as hell get their attention. He watched with satisfaction as the spread of phaser fire hit at various points on the ship.

"Their forward shields are damaged, sir," announced Worf, with perhaps just a hint of triumph. But it was Geordi's voice that cut in now. "We destroyed one of their phaser arrays . . . looks like collateral damage in the cargo area." Geordi scrutinized his sensor readings carefully, then said in an alarmed voice, "Sir, I'm picking up massive power fluctuations . . . internal explosions . . . with all the armament that ship is carrying—it's going to blow!"

Even with that warning, Riker wasn't prepared for what happened next.

The dark ship exploded in a cataclysmic eruption of flame and fire. Secondary explosions followed one after the other in a succession of towering blasts; extruded matter was hurled hundreds of kilometers into space. The catastrophic explosions continued until the viewers on the *Enterprise* could not imagine there being any matter left to detonate, but the molten core continued to erupt, spewing still more slabs of burning metal.

When it was over, there was nothing left. It was as though every bit of matter in the ship had been pulverized. Small flaming chunks drifted toward them, brought into sharp relief by the ship's sensors, though they were still thousands of kilometers away. Those last blazing embers gradually extinguished and became dust, and presently, there was only darkness and the undisturbed starfield.

It was as though the ship had never existed.

Chapter Nine

"WELL, MR. DATA—what do you think?"

They were still in their cramped quarters aboard the Klingon ship *Kruge.* Picard passed a mirror to Data, who took it and held it in front of him.

The reflection he saw revealed a startling transformation. Most immediately noticeable was the hue of his skin, which had lost its android paleness and was now an earthy, ruddy tone. His yellow eyes had been changed, with lenses, to a medium brown, and a prosthesis gave his skull and forehead the angular bony structure of the Romulans; a blunt-cut hairpiece completed the effect.

The cleverness of Beverly Crusher's prosthetics had become apparent when Picard and Data applied their Romulan ears. Made of a synthetic biopolymer material, they were able to mold directly into the skin with gentle pressure. No seam line was visible; they were as natural looking as their own ears.

Data took a full minute to inspect himself, and finally announced, "I am very pleased, sir. I would not have thought it possible." Picard admitted to himself that he had shared the same anxieties, and he breathed a silent thanks to Beverly for her expertise.

His own changeover had been as successful, he felt, and though the synthetic ears continued to give him a vaguely uncomfortable feeling, he was sure he would grow accustomed to them. He had been startled at first by seeing himself with hair; it had been a long time since he'd had a full head, and looking in the mirror was rather like looking at a portrait of himself as a young man.

They were both dressed in Romulan clothing, Data in a gray, square-cut jacket and Picard in a brown cape with a stand-away collar—replicated for them from accurate designs provided by Starfleet Command.

"I am eager to test the success of our efforts, sir. It does remain to be seen if the Romulans will accept us."

Picard smiled. "We'll soon find out," he replied. He knew that Data was incapable of feeling either eagerness or apprehension, yet he seemed to have something that passed for one of those emotions. Picard knew exactly what his fellow officer meant—he, too, was glad that the waiting was over and they were nearing Romulus. Biding time was difficult; Picard had no doubt that the several days of inactivity on the Klingon ship had helped to contribute to his aberrant dreams. He hoped, now that they were about to launch into the heart of the mission, those dreams would abate.

In the dreams, Sarek never appeared, and yet Picard knew he was there, lurking behind some vaporous curtain, just out of comprehension. Every morning,

Picard would wake shivering and chilled, remembering almost nothing of his dreams except the sensation of cold and a near avalanche of overwhelming emotion. Occasionally he would come to consciousness with the name of Perrin on his lips.

In each of those dreams, he dreaded the thought that Sarek might appear and he would have to look into those tortured dark eyes once more.

"Sir," said Data, "you have seemed unusually pensive since we received the news of Ambassador Sarek's death."

Picard began packing away the materials Beverly had provided them to complete their Romulan transformations. He knew what Data had said was true. He had felt himself turn inward when he read that message on K'Vada's padd; he had not wanted to examine or to talk about the effect that Sarek's death produced in him. Now Data's calm observation asked him to reflect on it.

"Sarek and I shared a particular bond," he began. "Our lives touched in an unusual way. I admit that I feel the effects of his loss."

Even as he spoke these words, Picard realized that he was intellectualizing the response, analyzing the situation and presenting a nonemotional reply. He tried to obscure the acknowledgment that he had no desire as yet to explore his feelings about the matter.

"The tenor of our mission has changed, at least for me," he continued, beginning to feel on safer ground by shifting the discussion away from himself and onto their journey. "We were sent to confront Spock about his disappearance. Now, we must also tell him his father is dead."

"I am afraid I do not entirely understand, sir. As a Vulcan, would not Ambassador Spock simply see death as a logical result of his father's illness?"

"It is never quite that simple. Not even for a Vulcan. Certainly not for Spock, who is also half human." Talking about Spock and Sarek certainly was more comfortable than talking about his own ambiguous relationship with them, and he tried not to listen to the nagging voice in his mind that told him he was avoiding something significant. "They spent a lifetime in conflict . . . now the chance to resolve their differences is gone."

Data took a moment to process this statement. "Considering the exceptionally long lifespan of the Vulcans," he said presently, "it does seem odd that Spock and Sarek did not choose to resolve those differences in the time available."

"Yes," acknowledged Picard. "It really is quite—illogical." He looked at Data, envied him briefly for the fact that he would forever remain innocent of the tangled agonies of human emotion. "A father and son . . . both proud, both stubborn . . . more alike than either would care to admit. They can't easily break down the emotional barriers they've spent a lifetime building."

Picard closed the satchel containing Beverly's implements. "And then the time comes when it is too late to try. When one realizes that all the things he had planned to say will go unsaid."

He looked into Data's guileless face, and wondered if the android grasped even a part of what he was saying. "That is a difficult moment. And a lonely one. Spock will now have to face that moment."

Data tilted his head in an effort to understand the

complex undertones of familial relationships. Picard felt a draft of cold air and turned to see what had caused it.

But as he suspected, nothing was there.

When Captain K'Vada saw the two Starfleet officers walk onto his bridge disguised as Romulans, he could not help but laugh. He thought they looked absurd, but then he thought Romulans themselves looked ridiculous, with their pointed ears, upswept eyebrows, and strange-colored skin.

"Don't you two look sweet?" he chortled at the two of them. Picard accepted the jibe without responding, as usual, and the android never changed expression. K'Vada couldn't resist pushing it a little further. He strolled toward Data and circled him, eyeing him up and down. "Be careful, android," he murmured. "Some Romulan beauty might take a liking to you . . . lick that paint right off your ears . . ." He was pleased to see that the now brown eyes blinked a bit at that.

Enjoying the discomfiture he felt he was creating, K'Vada moved to Picard, gave him a scrutinizing glance. "You know what the Romulans would do to you if they found you out?"

"I have a pretty good idea," replied Picard.

K'Vada wondered if he did. If he himself had not seen the results of a Romulan interrogation, he would not have believed it.

Picard eyed him coldly and announced, "We are ready to be transported to the surface, Captain." The brusque tone of his voice grated on K'Vada. He thought the Starfleet officer needed to be reminded of his place on this ship.

"Just so we understand each other," he said in a

voice he hoped was just dark enough to be menacing, "my orders don't include rescue missions."

For the first time, he saw something harden in Picard's eyes; it affected him more than a raised hand might from another man. K'Vada looked right into those flinty eyes, and after a moment convinced himself that he'd frightened Picard enough. He gestured casually to his tactical officer. "yIghuHlup!" he ordered. Then he turned back to Picard and Data. "Good luck, Captain," he said without rancor, and gestured once more. The two false Romulans dematerialized in front of him.

You'll need it and then some, he thought. Then he turned and sat in his command chair, and decided to devote the next hour to erotic thoughts of K'kam.

Chapter Ten

THE PLANET OF Romulus had throbbed below them like a live bacillus.

A planet could not throb, of course, but that's what it had seemed like to Picard as they had looked at it from the bridge of the *Kruge*. It was a gray, bleak sphere, from which occasional and spectacular eruptions of red fire blistered their way toward the upper atmosphere—the famed Firefalls of Gath Gal'thong. This massive area of constant volcanic activity was one aspect of Romulan geology that had become known outside their binary star system. On the unstable continent of Dektenb, tectonic plates ground and shifted against each other, and the molten interior of the planet sought the weak points of the crust. Flareups were frequent and immense, as plumes of flame shot miles into the sky; fires and lava flows glowed red and orange in serpentine patterns.

From space, the effect was that Romulus appeared to throb with malevolent, palpitating life.

Romulus was the third planet of a binary star

system comprised of Romulus and Romii. All the planets maintained a highly elliptical orbit; for that reason, geologic development was erratic. Dektenb was unpredictable and volatile; in the other hemisphere, the continent of Masfarik was barren and rocky except in a few oases where cities and towns struggled for survival. The population of the planet was jammed into these cities, which tended to grow upward rather than outward, and population density reached intolerable levels.

But if the planet, from space, throbbed with malignant, pulsing life, there was no sense of that muscular vitality on the streets of the capital city of Dartha. Now that he and Data had transported to the surface, and into the teeming neighborhood known as Krocton segment, Picard was overwhelmed with a sense of deadness. Massive structures of steel and glass climbed toward the skies, creating narrow tunnels below where sunlight seemed not to penetrate. An eternal dusk prevailed, relieved sporadically by artificial lights that had been installed at periodic intervals and whose pale green light seemed ineffectual against the relentless gloom.

At street level there was no evidence of steel or glass. Dartha was an ancient city, and had grown upward from the ground. Here at its lower depths the foundations were of timeworn granite, stained with age and use. The harsh angles of the architecture were punctuated with occasional touches of strange whimsy; Picard noted two leering creatures like gargoyles carved in stone, peering down from a high lintel.

But the most desolate component of the city was its people.

Dressed in dark, drab clothing, they moved along

the streets with heads down, rarely speaking, not even making eye contact. No one seemed in a hurry, no one seemed even to have a purpose; clumps of them would stand on corners, congregated for no apparent reason or function. Some spoke in low tones, but there was no sense of joy, of ambition, not even of anger. There was only an overriding pall of grim despair.

Picard knew that life was difficult in Krocton segment, and everyone very much looked out for themselves. They would have to be constantly vigilant; this was not a situation in which they could expect any quarter given. He recalled ancient laboratory experiments in which rats were crowded into smaller and smaller cages; eventually, stripped of space, they began eating each other.

He and Data stood quietly for a few moments, inspecting the situation. They attracted no attention by doing so, for many others stood silently in the same way. Picard saw Data gazing ingenuously at the surroundings, and knew that he was memorizing every detail.

Picard drew his cloak about him more closely. He wasn't cold; in fact, Dartha was exceptionally warm. Perhaps he was trying to keep the insidious spirit of hopelessness from invading his soul.

Proconsul Neral of Romulus stood at the windows of his office and gazed contentedly at the spectacular views. In the foreground, the city spires rose proudly toward the skies; beyond them, dark, jagged mountains erputed in fierce grandeur. Neral loved those mountains, and would spend long moments staring out at them, enjoying their majestic, dreadful beauty.

Such views were rare in Dartha; only the upper

echelons of the Romulan hierarchy could aspire to them. His office, likewise, was large, and stately, with a quiet elegance. The marble fixtures, the exquisitely tooled leather chairs, the massive, hand-carved desk —all these amenities were comforting to him. He worked hard on behalf of the Romulan people; he felt justified in enjoying the environment in which he did that work.

The door opened and Neral smiled pleasantly at the rotund figure who entered. "Ah, Senator Pardek. You received my message."

"I got here as quickly as I could, proconsul."

Neral smiled and gestured toward the monitor on his desk. "What do you know of this human, Jean-Luc Picard?"

Pardek looked puzzled. "Picard," he repeated.

"Yes. Have you seen him recently?"

"To my knowledge, I've never seen him."

"I have received intelligence that says he's on his way here. Perhaps here already," Neral said.

This produced a truly surprised response. Pardek looked amazed as he responded, "Here—on Romulus?"

"Yes. Curious, isn't it? I suppose we'd better find out if the report is accurate—or merely rumor." Neral eyed the old senator briefly, considering his next move. "Circulate his likeness to the security forces," he ordered. "Remind them that if he *is* here, he is probably disguised as one of us."

"I'll see to it," said Pardek, and scurried toward the door. Relieved that Pardek was taking this disquieting responsibility from him, Neral turned once more to contemplate the stark beauty of the black mountains.

* * *

Picard felt as though they had been standing in the same place for an hour, though he knew that only minutes had passed. Time in this dank, dreary place seemed elongated, as though the unpleasant minutes moved more slowly. When Data spoke to him, he felt jolted from a reverie.

"This is definitely the street on which the intelligence scan of Spock and Pardek was taken, sir. Adjusting for the optical distortion, I am able to verify the architectural features."

"Where were they standing?" asked Picard. That might offer them a clue as to where to start looking for either Pardek or Spock. He waited while Data did some processing, looking up and down the street. Picard was afraid that his movements seemed too androidlike and might attract attention. He stepped toward him and casually draped his arm around Data's shoulder. "Data," he began.

"Yes?"

"You're moving about in a very—android manner."

"I am sorry, Captain," replied Data immediately. "I will be more careful."

"And don't call me 'Captain.'"

"Yes, Cap—" Data cut himself off. "I understand."

Then, looking around in as human a manner as he could summon, he said, "I have located the spot where they were standing."

Picard removed his arm from Data's shoulders. He realized that such camaraderie was not typical of the Romulans. "Where?" he asked.

To his surprise, Data now put *his* arm around Picard's shoulders and led him a few doors down the street. "It is here," he said. "At this doorway."

Picard looked at a small sign near the door, which, being written in Romulan, was indecipherable to him. To his relief, Data dropped his arm and moved forward to read the sign. "A legal intercessor's office," he announced. "The name is similar to Pardek's. It would appear to be one of his relatives."

Picard reached out and tried the door; it didn't yield. "Not open for business yet," he guessed.

"Nevertheless," Data ventured, "it would be my recommendation that we keep this location under observation. I have clearly determined Pardek's routine. On days when the Senate is not in session, he invariably comes to this section after the median hour."

Picard quickly glanced around, looking for a reason they could stay close to this office without attracting attention. He saw, within close range, people eating at a cluster of tables—a *dinglh,* or food center. He turned back to Data. "Very well, why don't we take the opportunity to try some of the local cuisine."

They moved casually toward the food court, passing as they did some Romulan soldiers. They were hard-looking men who strolled indolently along the street; Picard and Data kept their eyes straight ahead, and had no idea if the soldiers took notice of their passing.

Every patron of the food court was standing at the small tables that dotted it. Picard and Data did the same, and were immediately approached by a dour woman with small, piercing eyes. She inspected them carefully.

"What do you recommend?" asked Data easily.

"Soup," was her terse reply.

"That sounds very appealing," Data assured her. "I will have soup."

The woman's stern look swung to Picard. "Soup is fine," he said.

She moved off and Picard turned nonchalantly and glanced toward the soldiers. They were still nearby, talking in hushed tones. He turned back and saw the woman approaching them with two bowls. Picard looked at her and asked in a friendly voice, "Do you know what time the intercessor's office across the way opens?"

"Why do you want to know?" Her voice was flat.

"I need his services. He was recommended."

There was a brief pause, and then the woman said, "I haven't seen you here before."

"We are here for the day," Data interjected smoothly. "From the city of Rateg."

"Rateg," she said. "I don't think so."

Picard tried to stay calm. If this woman was suspicious, and the soldiers only a few feet away . . .

"Why do you say that?" asked Data.

"You don't sound like you're from Rateg."

"Ah," said Data, on sure ground here, "it is a misconception that all Rategs speak with a particular inflection. In fact, there are twelve different—"

"We come from several kilometers outside the city," interrupted Picard evenly. If Data got into the detailed complexities of his voluminous research, they would be quickly uncovered.

The woman drew back and studied them for a moment. "Or perhaps," she offered, "you come from the security forces, to watch the intercessor's office. Is he in trouble?"

"Madame, you are mistaken." Picard was genuinely surprised.

"It doesn't matter to me," she shrugged. "I don't know when he opens. Eat your soup. Courtesy of a loyal establishment. *Jolan tru.*"

She moved off and Picard breathed a silent sigh of relief. He noted that Data was already drinking the broth that the woman had set before them. He looked down at his own. It was a thin, greasy gruel with a rancid smell. He had read of this popular dish, *gletten,* in his research, and wished now he had not. It didn't help to know what was in it.

He took a sip and, as he did, looked up to see that the soldiers had been looking at them; when he glanced up, they quickly turned their heads.

Picard took another swallow of the distasteful liquid, and then said quietly to Data, "We can't stay here long."

"We may not have to," Data answered. "Direct your view to the far corner. Is that not Pardek?"

The bowl to his lips, Picard shifted his glance in the direction Data had indicated. There, just having entered the area, was a round-faced man in a brown cloak, moving to talk with several people clustered together. He had the same kindly visage as the man they had seen on the Barolian tape.

"I believe you're right," said Picard. He set down the bowl and concentrated on watching Pardek. But he heard Data's voice in his ear. "Perhaps you should appear to enjoy your soup."

He turned and realized that the foot soldiers were staring at them again. With a subtle show of enjoyment, Picard lifted the bowl and drank deeply. As he swallowed the slightly gelatinous broth, he noted that it was undoubtedly a far easier task for Data to feign enthusiasm for this dreadful mixture. He realized he'd better stop thinking about it or he might not be able to finish it.

Uneasily, he noticed that the foot soldiers had moved into the food center and were now standing only a few meters behind them, talking easily. Picard kept his eyes on Pardek, who now bid farewell to his colleagues and began to move further on down the street.

Picard and Data unceremoniously put down their bowls and turned to move after him.

But the soldiers were right there, blocking their way, disruptors drawn. "Do not move," said one.

Picard was aware that the patrons of the food court had drawn imperceptibly away, heads down, ignoring the confrontation as though it weren't happening. "What is it?" demanded Picard. "You've made a mistake."

"Quiet," said the other soldier, his voice menacing. "Come with us."

Strong hands grabbed them and shoved them up the street, and within minutes they were sitting inside an antigrav pod, streaking along the labyrinthine streets of Dartha, toward a fate that Picard was sure would be unpleasant.

Picard's sense of alarm was heightened when he realized the soldiers' vehicle was taking them out of the city. This did not portend well. The proconsul's secret security forces were known for their ability to extract information from spies, and it seemed not unreasonable that there were particular locations for such activities. Captain K'Vada's dire warning flashed uncomfortably through Picard's mind.

When they disembarked at the mouth of a cave, his dark suspicions grew stronger. The soldiers prodded them into a tunnel lit at intervals by the intense white light of kekogen lamps. Picard knew that, within the bowels of this cave, one could scream for days on end and never be heard except by those whose ministrations he suffered.

The soldiers pushed them down a ramp, at the bottom of which was a subterranean chamber of some size. There was a small group of Romulans assembled in the room, and Picard noted briefly that they seemed to be civilians; that seemed anomalous.

"Wait here," said the soldier gruffly.

"For what?" asked Picard, hoping the challenge would help to still the heightened beating of his heart.

But there was no answer. The soldiers watched them carefully, disruptors still aimed; the civilians regarded them curiously.

Then there was a sudden movement at the top of the ramp, and everyone in the vaulted chamber turned toward it.

Pardek strolled down the ramp, his cheerful face somehow out of place in these dark surroundings. "Welcome to Romulus, Captain Picard."

Picard's mind reeled, embracing the possibilities. He didn't want to speak before he had his bearings in this unexpected circumstance. He saw that the Romulan soldiers were now stripping off their uniforms—revealing civilian clothing underneath.

"Don't let our 'soldiers' alarm you," said Pardek.

"We had to get you off the streets quickly. Romulan security knows you are here."

Picard looked quickly around the room, trying to assess the situation. Were these people an underground movement of some kind? One that operated with Pardek's support and approval? Or was this some kind of ruse, intended to throw him off balance and force him to reveal his true purpose?

Pardek's voice was reassuring. "I am Pardek. You are among friends, Captain."

He looked into the man's eyes and knew he must take the risk. He had not come across three sectors to Romulus and into the midst of the Federation's enemies because he intended to play it safely. The stakes were too high for that.

"I have come on an urgent mission from the Federation," he announced. "I am looking for Ambassador Spock."

There was silence.

Then, from the depths of the cavern, through a tunnel shrouded in darkness, came a voice.

"Indeed," it said.

All heads turned toward the sound.

Footsteps began to echo on the cave floor, emanating from deep within the tunnel, the measured steps ringing with amazing magnitude in the silence of the cave.

The steps grew closer. Picard strained to see into the tunnel, but there was only gloom. The footsteps echoed louder and louder in the stillness.

Then a shadowy figure began to emerge, a tall person, regal and poised, his face still shrouded in darkness. The man stepped into the light.

111

It was Spock.

"You have found him, Captain Picard," he intoned.

There was no warmth to his voice, and his piercing eyes were cold. He stared at the man who had traveled so far to see him, but there was no welcome in the look.

Chapter Eleven

WHAT SEEMED LIKE several minutes passed in a strange kind of suspension. Picard was aware of the hushed silence of the onlookers, the eerie glow cast by the kekogen lamps in the cave, of Data's curious gaze and Pardek's puckish face in the shadows. He was aware of all those things.

But he *saw* only Spock's eyes.

Dark and probing, they held Picard's in a look that caused him to feel the blood pounding in his head. There was no outward indication of anger; Spock's face was expressionless. But those eyes were black fire, a window to some deep and unfathomable part of the man where anger churned and seethed.

Picard was fascinated, held in that grip like a bird mesmerized by a snake's eye. It was not until Spock uttered his next words that Picard felt released from the hold of that powerful gaze.

"What are you doing on Romulus?" No preamble, no niceties, just blunt frontal assault. But the words restored Picard to a sense of himself, and when he spoke, his voice was clear and calm.

"That was to be my question for you, sir."

"It is no concern of Starfleet's."

"On the contrary, Starfleet is most concerned." Picard was finding the dialectic comfortable; debate put him on familiar ground. "You are in a position to compromise the security of the Federation."

Spock's look hardened. "You may assure your superiors that I am on a personal mission of peace, and will advise them when appropriate."

Picard's voice echoed Spock's resoluteness. "That will not be satisfactory." And he saw a flash in Spock's eye, felt the conflict growing, knew they were polarizing.

"You *cannot* remain, Captain," retorted Spock, as though that final statement ended the dispute.

"And I cannot return without a full explanation." Picard took a breath, then plunged ahead. "Ambassador, with the greatest respect for all you've achieved on behalf of the Federation, this sort of cowboy diplomacy is not easily tolerated any more."

Picard noted that he had scored with that. Spock seemed almost amazed as he repeated, *"Cowboy* diplomacy?"

"If you wish to undertake a mission with potential repercussions to the Federation, it is appropriate to discuss it with the Federation. I am here as their representative. You will have to discuss it with me. Now."

Spock moved away from him, frowning with frustration. "This is precisely what I wanted to avoid."

Picard felt Spock's backing off was perhaps an effort to constrain rising emotions. He sensed it was time to move from confrontation, although he was reluctant to introduce the next subject. But it had to come.

"I also have the responsibility of bearing some unhappy news."

Spock turned back and fixed him with those penetrating eyes.

"Sarek is dead," he said.

Startled, Picard thought for a moment that the news had reached Romulus somehow, then realized that it was simply Spock's prescience.

There was a long silence. Picard could hear others breathing, shifting position, feeling uncomfortable about the nakedness of this intimate moment. Finally, Spock gestured toward a passageway.

"Walk with me, Captain Picard."

Picard glanced at Data, letting him know it was all right to stay behind, and followed Spock out of the chamber. They walked quietly through the rough pathway and then emerged into another, smaller section, one where water oozed from the walls and dripped into unseen underground rivers. It was warm and moist there, and Picard was reminded of the vineyards of southern France just before a thunderstorm.

Spock turned and gazed at him. Whatever might be going on inside him, there was no hint of it on the surface. His voice, when he spoke, was as composed as ever. "I know of your mind meld with my father. It enabled him to complete his last mission."

"It was an honor. He was a great man."

"He was a great representative of the Vulcan people and of the Federation."

Picard gave him a glance. It sounded as though Spock meant that as a qualifier, and not a compliment. But with his dry intonation, it was impossible to be sure.

Picard thought of Sarek, a feeble, trembling man with tears staining his face, unable to hold his hand in the Vulcan salute. His last words were a plea to Picard to convey to his son what he felt, but now in Spock's presence Picard felt inadequate to the task. How to tell Spock of Sarek's love for him? How to convey a lifetime of feelings unspoken? Yet he felt bound to try.

"I was with him before coming here," he began. "He expressed his pride in you, his love . . ." The words sounded hollow in Picard's ears, and his mind struggled to find better ones.

"Emotional disarray," replied Spock dryly, "is a symptom of the illness from which he suffered."

"No, the feelings were in his heart, Spock. He shared them with me. I know."

Spock turned away and Picard knew he was uncomfortable with this emotional discussion. He would prefer to mourn Sarek's death in his own way, some rational acknowledgment that all living beings die; Picard was making him uneasy with the message from his father.

Spock moved back to business. "Sarek would no more approve of my coming to Romulus than you do, Captain." He began to pace the small, humid chamber, organizing his thoughts, gradually becoming caught up in his ideas, eager to communicate.

"For some time, I have been aware of a growing movement here . . . of people who seek to learn the ideals of the Vulcan philosophy. They have been declared enemies of the state. But there are a few in the Romulan hierarchy, like Pardek, who are sympathetic." Spock paused and looked solemnly at Picard.

And then he said something that Picard would never, in his wildest thoughts, have imagined to have been at the heart of Spock's clandestine journey to Romulus: "He asked me to come here now because he believes it may be time to take the first step toward reunification."

Picard stared at him, genuinely stunned at this revelation. His mind whirled to process the ramifications. "Reunification . . . after so many centuries . . . so many fundamental differences that have evolved between your peoples . . ."

"It would seem unlikely to succeed," Spock agreed. "But I cannot ignore the potential rewards that a union between our worlds would bring."

Picard took a moment to reflect. He was familiar with the history of the Vulcans and Romulans, who were once one people—a passionate, raging, violent race whose emotions were untrammeled. The Vulcans, fearing the consequences of unbridled sensibilities, consciously opted for a life of control and orderliness, a life in which meditation was used to conquer rampant feelings, a life of contemplation in which reason and logic were lifted to an exalted position.

The Romulans made no such effort. Their passions raged unchecked. They were violent, turbulent, vicious, and cruel. They channeled their native intelligence into warfare and conquest, their productivity into armament and weapons—instruments of death.

Centuries had passed since the original separation. Was it possible, after all that time, that the two nations could find a rebirth in unification? Picard's mind scrambled to understand the nuances of this monumental plan.

"What is this 'first step' that Pardek suggests?"

"There is a new proconsul of the Romulan Senate, Neral. He is young and idealistic. He has promised many reforms. Pardek believes he may be receptive to discussing reunification."

Picard digested this. "Why would you not bring something this important to the attention of your people—or the Federation?"

He could see Spock's mind reeling backwards—one hundred thirty years of memories, how could one contain them all?—and light on a painful incident. "A personal decision, Captain. Perhaps you are aware that I played a small role in the first overture to peace with the Klingons . . ."

"History is aware of the role you played, Ambassador."

"Not entirely. It was I who asked Kirk to lead that peace mission. And I who had to accept the responsibility for the consequences to him and his crew." Spock's dark eyes held his for a brief moment. "Quite simply, I am unwilling to risk anyone's life but my own on this occasion. I would ask you to respect my wishes and leave."

Picard had to suppress a smile. "Ambassador, your logic escapes me. If I didn't know better, I would say your judgment had been influenced by emotion."

There was a new timbre to Spock's voice as he replied. "You speak as my father would if he were here, Picard."

Hearing the bite to that speech, Picard retorted in kind. "I speak as a Starfleet officer. And I cannot ignore the risks to you—"

"I was involved with 'cowboy diplomacy,' as you

describe it, Captain, long before you were born," Spock came back. They were polarizing again.

"Nevertheless, sir, I am not prepared to leave until your affairs are completed."

Spock hurled him a look of withering disdain. "In your own way, you are as stubborn as another captain of the *Enterprise* I once knew."

Picard repressed the smile. "Then, sir," he stated calmly, "I am in good company."

Spock stared at him for what felt like an hour and was probably only seconds. Finally, he nodded— which Picard was only too glad to take as acquiescence.

Chapter Twelve

CAPTAIN K'VADA'S SHOULDER was not healing well. At night he suffered awfully and could not find any position in which the lancing pains did not interrupt his sleep. Each time he adjusted his body his shoulder felt as though a fiery brand were being jabbed into it, and he had to force himself not to cry out.

He would mutter vile oaths toward K'kam, willing the most ghastly catastrophies to befall her for having caused him this grief. When he saw her again he would punish her himself, and he briefly derived some satisfaction from a vision of K'kam, her strong, sinewy body glistening with sweat, begging him for mercy.

Days brought some relief from the pain, which seemed to ease with activity, but lack of sleep made him irritable, and his crew was beginning to dread his appearance on the bridge. He had already ordered disciplines for several and had had another locked in chains for several days without food or water. He had finally relented when he visited the wretch and found him near unconsciousness from thirst, his lips cracked and bleeding, but who refused nonetheless to beg for mercy. He glared at K'Vada with burning eyes, proudly silent, and K'Vada was moved by his courage.

Now K'Vada sat in his command chair, shoulder throbbing with each beat of his heart, and listened to what the absurd-looking Commander Data, still in his Romulan guise, was telling him.

And it made him even more irate.

The Starfleet creature was telling him that Picard was remaining on the surface for an undetermined amount of time, and that the *Kruge* would be required to stay in orbit, cloaked, until such time as he chose to return.

K'Vada glared at Data. "We have more important things to attend to than acting as your nursemaids," he grumbled.

Data's voice was annoyingly calm. "Captain Picard regrets that he must detain you but it is necessary for a while longer. In addition, I will be requiring access to your ship's computer."

This statement caused K'Vada to lean forward abruptly, and he winced as a fierce pain lanced through his shoulder. "Access to our computer? For what purpose?"

"I am going to attempt to penetrate the Romulan central information net."

In spite of the misery of his shoulder, K'Vada smiled. "Don't bother," he warned. "We've been trying for years."

"I have unique skills that may permit me to succeed."

The nagging suspicion that that was true annoyed K'Vada. He felt compelled to offer obstacles. "I cannot reveal classified Klingon entry codes to Starfleet."

"Your entry codes can be easily reconfigured after we depart." *With great effort,* thought K'Vada, and was prepared to refuse permission until Data added, "And Captain Picard has authorized me to share with you any information we obtain from the Romulan data banks."

Captain K'Vada frowned and grunted, but his mind was giddy with the prospect of tapping into Romulan intelligence. This would bring him praise and commendation from the High Council. Romulan data banks! Never had the Klingons had such information. His mind accommodated a brief image of K'kam, in awe of her remarkable mate, aroused and growling, promising him any pleasure he wanted . . .

"Anything *else?*" he asked sarcastically, still trying to save face.

To his surprise, the android replied, "We will also need to communicate with the *Enterprise* in sector two-thirteen."

"You do and the Romulans will instantly know our coordinates," shot back K'Vada. Was the android mad? Surely he knew there could be no communication out of the Neutral Zone.

But Data's equanimity was undisturbed. "Using conventional means, that would be true; however, I propose that we piggyback our signal on Romulan subspace transmissions."

"Piggyback?" K'Vada had never heard the phrase; it sounded faintly silly.

"A human metaphor—pardon me. We would use a

Romulan signal as a carrier for our own, thus disguising its origin."

It was a stunningly simple idea. K'Vada cursed inwardly that it had never occurred to him. "It won't work," he announced.

"I believe it will." The android, unaffected by K'Vada's curt reply, proceeded to explain his rationale with measured calm. "During the last hour, I have conducted a systematic review of the entire Romulan subspace grid and compared my findings with the specifications of your transmission array. It would appear they are compatible."

K'Vada studied him for a long moment. Something had occurred to him, something that was likely to bring him even more honor than information from the Romulan data banks. He brusquely nodded his approval to Data, who politely replied, "Thank you for your cooperation," then exited the bridge.

K'Vada turned his new thought over in his mind for a few moments, and it was sweet. Almost smiling now, he moved to a comm panel and tapped in his entry code. "Captain's notation," he said confidently. "Recommend we study the potential for a Klingon artificial life entity."

He had mused on the idea for several moments before he realized that his shoulder had stopped aching.

Spock saw the boy from the corner of his eye, running down the street, already out of breath, clutching the rose-colored *lagga* flower in his fist. It was D'Tan, a Romulan child not yet past puberty. Spock recognized him from his whippet body and smooth, gaited run; he had marveled at the boy's boundless energy on several occasions. *That is one thing age gives us,* he thought. *An appreciation of things the young take for granted.*

D'Tan paused near a line of Romulans who were queued for a goods dispenser, and handed the flower to one of the men standing there—a man Spock knew as Jaron.

The man took the flower, glanced furtively around, then stepped out of line. Spock knew Jaron was headed toward him, but he kept his eyes resolutely forward.

Spock and Picard were standing at one of the small tables that dotted the floor of the *dinglh.* They had been standing casually there for several minutes and had already ordered soup—almost the only thing that was ever available. Spock knew that the powerful denizens of Romulus dined each night on sumptuous delicacies; the ordinary man stood in line for a crown of bread and a chunk of gristle.

Spock would have preferred to be here alone; he had hoped to convince Picard to transport back to his Klingon ship and then return to Federation space. An affair like this was best handled without outside interference and with as few participants as possible. The delicacy of the situation made a Starfleet captain's presence troubling, indeed.

Spock looked at the trim, fit man opposite him, registered his grave, intelligent eyes and his assured bearing, and reflected that, all his misgivings notwithstanding, if Starfleet felt they had to send someone, this had undoubtedly been a wise choice.

He had never met Jean-Luc Picard, but he had of course heard of the captain of the fleet's flagship. His reputation heralded him as a man of courage, erudition, and compassion, and in their brief encounter Spock had no reason to doubt any of those qualities. To those he might add perceptivity, articulateness, and tenacity.

All the same, he made Spock uneasy. And he wasn't sure why.

Spock disliked not being able to objectify his instinct; it was like an elusive mote in the eye that can't be seen or extracted but continues to irritate nonetheless. What was it about Picard that he found so disquieting?

Perhaps it was that Picard's attitude about the possibility of unification was simply not logical. Spock was sure that the Federation and its representatives could only benefit if his mission were successful, and he did not doubt that Picard would ultimately be supportive of such a movement. So there was no reason for Picard to disapprove of his goal.

But he did. That was it—Jean-Luc Picard thought he was an impressionable fool for having entered into this endeavor.

Perhaps that is why Spock seemed to hear his father's voice whenever Picard voiced his concerns about the reunification talks. Sarek, too, had never given credence to Spock's beliefs that there were some Romulans who wanted peace, who wanted to live in reborn harmony with their Vulcan cousins. It had been a lifelong source of conflict. And now here was this Picard, echoing that same attitude.

In a way, it was fascinating.

In a corner of the *dinglh,* Spock saw the man with the flower moving idly toward them. In a moment he was passing their table, and as he did so he casually placed the blossom in a glass of water, then deposited it in front of Spock.

"Allow me to brighten your table," Jaron intoned, and Spock nodded noncommittally. *"Jolan tru,"* added the man, and moved on. The Romulan greeting, which meant variously "good day," "best wishes," or "good luck," was a neutral one shared by all. It connoted no political allegiance or leaning, though Spock knew the man was a member of the movement.

He turned back toward Picard, his voice quiet; fortunately, a hushed conversation drew no attention, for everyone spoke in guarded tones in this city. "The Senate has adjourned. Pardek will be here shortly." He glanced toward the pink *lagga* blossom. "The flower is a signal."

Picard nodded. Spock knew the Starfleet captain was curious to hear Pardek's message, for it would signal either an end to or a continuation of Spock's objective. Picard's eyes carefully swept the interior of the food center; Spock was pleased that he was ever on the alert. "Just how widespread is this movement?" asked the captain.

They had been talking, before D'Tan's flower had arrived, about the remarkable events that were transpiring here in the Romulan system. Picard had listened carefully, gathering in the information Spock provided him, asking intelligent questions. He seemed to be intrigued by Spock's revelation of an active, pervasive underground of those who longed for reunification. "I am told," replied Spock, "that there are groups in every populated area."

He stopped as he felt the arrival of the matron; he had not seen her here before and was unwilling to take the chance that even a whispered conversation might be overheard. The woman sat before them bowls of *gletten,* eyed the flower, looked hard at them, and then moved off.

"The spread of these groups has become a serious concern to the Romulan leadership," Spock then continued.

"Serious enough for the leaders to suddenly embrace a Vulcan peace initiative? I have a difficult time accepting that."

In that sentence, Spock heard the intransigence and stubbornness that disturbed him. He admired the fact that this captain had courage; he would never be intimidated into altering his position. But could he not embrace the possibility of change? Was he thoroughly inflexible?

"I sense you have a closed mind, Captain," he retorted. "Closed minds have kept these two worlds apart for centuries."

He saw Picard give him a look that suggested puzzlement. Perhaps he had spoken a bit sharply. Spock continued, determined to win his support. "In the Federation, we have learned from experience to view the Romulans with distrust. We can either choose to live with that enmity or seek an opportunity to change it." He paused and looked at Picard with his most penetrating gaze. "I choose the latter."

Picard seemed unaffected by the stare. "I will be the first to cheer when the Neutral Zone is abolished, sir. I only wonder if this movement is strong enough to reshape the entire Romulan political landscape."

Again, it was a familiar tone that Spock heard from this man. Surprising that it did something to his stomach that was vexatious.

His eyes shifted and fell on the flower in the glass, already wilted and gasping in the Romulan heat. "One can begin to reshape the landscape with a single flower, Captain."

He didn't look at Picard to see what response that observation had produced, because he had noticed D'Tan approaching, his wiry child's body full of angles and joints. He was carrying something.

"Jolan tru, Mr. Spock," he said. D'Tan always spoke as though he were half out of breath, probably because he never walked when he could run. "Look what I've brought you."

"This is my friend D'Tan," Spock told Picard. "He is very curious about Vulcan."

"Hello, D'Tan." Picard's voice was friendly, if somewhat cautious. Spock sensed a man who, though warmhearted, was not comfortable with children.

D'Tan handed Spock a book and he turned it in his hands. It was worn, with a cover made of wood that had been carved by hand, and pages that were smudged and brittle. "It is very old," ventured Spock. "Where did you get this?"

"They read from it at the meetings. It tells the story of the Vulcan separation—"

A new voice knifed into the conversation, startling them all. "You should not bring that out here, D'Tan. You've been told many times."

They turned to see Pardek approaching, his benign face a ruddy red from the heat. D'Tan looked sheepish and took possession of the book once more. "I just wanted to show it to Mr. Spock," he said lamely.

Pardek's smile was not threatening. "Off with you. We will see you later tonight."

D'Tan's eyes sought Spock's, as though to feed from .

him once more before he left. "Will you tell us more stories about Vulcan?" he asked.

"Yes," answered Spock, and enjoyed the smile that D'Tan gave him in return. Then the boy sprinted off, hurling back over his shoulder as he did, *"Jolan tru."*

Spock saw Pardek casting his practiced eye around the denizens of the food center and lighting on the grim-faced old woman who had brought their *gletten.* "Perhaps this is not such a good place to talk," he murmured, and the three moved casually out of the court and into the colorless world of the Romulan streets.

Spock knew that most of his countrymen, and most Federation members for that matter, would find the dark, somber passageways of this city bleak and depressing. Ironically, he did not. The vast, rugged beauty of Vulcan, with its ocher deserts and its jagged red mountains, had instilled in him a love of spaciousness and light. Why, then, his appreciation of these squalid passageways where little light intruded? The dark facades of the structures were ominous, the corridors narrow and constricting. The people all dressed in pallid clothing and their expressions were quietly despairing. There would seem to be little to cherish in these desolate streets.

But Spock had a palpable sense of the spirit that lurked beneath; a knowledge that, behind those joyless faces, burned the eagerness for a new order. There was a river of desire that ran unseen beneath this city, a wellspring from which more and more would soon be drinking. That such a flame could burn in these woeful alleyways seemed remarkable to him, and imbued the surroundings with a unique beauty whose essence was almost tangible to him.

The three men walked the street, heads down in Romulan fashion. Pardek cast a glance toward Picard. "And what do you think of your enemy, Captain Picard?"

Picard gave him a look that was not accusatory yet had an intensity that surprised Spock. "These people are no one's enemy, Senator." *How true,* thought Spock, *and if only someone would tell that to all the governmental authorities and all the military leaders. The people were rarely each other's enemies . . .*

Pardek smiled an acknowledgment. "Many of my colleagues fear what the people have to say. But I have learned to listen carefully." Pardek paused a moment, formulating his thoughts. "Children like D'Tan are our future. Old men like me will not be able to hold on to ancient prejudice and hostility. These young people won't allow it."

Spock glanced at Picard, to see what effect these words were having on him. Picard seemed to be listening intently.

"Now that they've met their first real Vulcan," continued Pardek, "it has only inspired them more. I'm sure that is evident to you, Spock."

"I did not anticipate such a passionate response to my arrival," admitted Spock, remembering the near delirious joy with which some people at meetings had greeted him.

Pardek smiled. "Romulans are a passionate people. Vulcans will learn to appreciate that quality in us."

"If we are successful," added Spock, curious that Pardek seemed so optimistic today. Were there new developments?

That question was answered an instant later when

Pardek looked at him with a smile that crinkled his merry eyes. "We will know soon," he declared, not without a certain pride. "The proconsul, Neral, has agreed to meet with you."

Spock was pleased to note that Picard seemed amazed by this announcement.

Chapter Thirteen

FOR RIKER, the week at Qualor Two had passed like a day. After the astonishing explosion of the smuggler's ship, the *Enterprise* had gone into synchronous orbit around the planet in order to investigate. Klim Dokachin had put the full resources of the formidable Zakdornian computer system at their disposal, as well as the combined sensibilities of several dozen of his colleagues to whom the desecration of their surplus depot was tantamount to sacrilege.

Riker found, after his initial period of discomfort with Dokachin's officiousness, that the rotund little man was a treasure. He had taken the theft of his ships and his materiel as a personal affront, and would leave nothing undone in order to uncover the perpetrator. The Zakdorn were methodical and fastidious to a fault, but in a case like this they were of inestimable value.

He and Gretchen Naylor had spent hours with Dokachin at a computer console, tracking manifests and logs. They had uncovered a trail of lost materiel that went back well over a year, and which included sensor arrays, deflectors, computers, armament, and almost anything else integral to the fitting of space-ships.

And then there were the two missing ships: the *T'Pau*, the quest for which had begun this whole adventure; and the *Tripoli*, the huge cargo ship that had been used to store equipment that was routinely stripped from starships consigned to the depot.

It was, reflected Riker, an ambitious and remarkably clever plan. The *Tripoli*—they weren't sure how yet—had quietly been slipped from its docking space. Whenever shipments were beamed to its coordinates, the smuggler's ship apparently took its place and received the goods, then warped away with no one the wiser.

"It seems to me that would mean there was a collaborator on the surface," mused Riker. They were on board the *Enterprise*, seated in one of the small security offices on Deck Nine; Riker was leaning back in his chair, absorbing the information Gretchen was relaying to him, mulling it over, worrying it like a pup with an old sock. "The computer would have to have been reconfigured to indicate the *Tripoli* was still there. Unless the locking coordinates were showing on the computer, whoever was programming the transport would have known there was nothing there."

Gretchen was nodding, her glossy black hair pulled back today into a thick braid. Riker noted idly that he liked that look on her. "I think there was someone else involved, too," she was saying. "So does Dokachin. He's written a scanning program to look for patterns in computer usage during the last year. He'll cross-reference the usage patterns with personal and duty logs to find who might be responsible."

Riker nodded his approval. "We need to find that person. They might be our only link to whoever it was that piloted the smuggler's ship."

"Dokachin will transport on board at fifteen hundred hours," said Gretchen. "Maybe he'll have some results by then."

"That leaves time for lunch," said Riker, realizing that it had been hours since breakfast. "Join me?"

"We have a replicator in the conference room," offered Gretchen. "We can eat and continue to study files." She rose and Riker grinned as he got to his feet. Naylor set a pace that few could match; she was single-minded in her diligence. He wondered if she was always this absorbed in her work. If so, he doubted that she had any friendships, male or female, for there would be literally no time to formulate them.

He also realized that for all the hours they had spent together this week, he knew remarkably little about her. She was friendly and cheerful, but other than sharing first names, they had exchanged no other personal information. Riker decided to do something about that.

She ate sensibly, as he somehow knew she would: a vegetable salad and rice bread; he opted for an omelet even though he'd never quite adapted to the taste of replicated eggs.

"I'd rather have them fresh," he admitted, and she looked at him in mild surprise.

"You mean—cook?" she queried.

"I enjoy cooking. Not all the time, mind you, but I make a mean omelet myself."

"With what?" She sounded genuinely mystified.

"With whatever I can find . . . eggs, vegetables, that kind of thing. It doesn't happen often." He was silent for a moment, dousing catsup on the omelet. Replicated catsup was even stranger than eggs, but somehow the two complemented each other.

"I've never cooked," she stated flatly. "My mother didn't cook. No one in my *family* has ever cooked. I don't understand—it just seems like a waste of time."

He smiled. This was not an uncommon attitude. In fact, it was becoming rarer and rarer to find anybody —especially in Starfleet—who had ever participated in any kind of food preparation. "To me, it's a creative outlet. Every time I make something, I try to vary it a little, so it never comes out the same way twice."

"Why?" Her brow was knotted in a frown.

He shrugged. "Aren't there things you just like to do . . . for no reason except that it gives you pleasure?"

She considered. "I like to work. That gives me pleasure."

"I mean besides work. Music, art, reading, sports . . ." He paused, remembering the fragrant hills of her home, and offered, "Gardening."

"Definitely not that. I saw enough of gardens in Indiana to last me all my life." She looked up at him and smiled, and he could see flecks of another color— gold?—in her eyes. "You have to realize, I knew from the time I was a little girl that I wanted Starfleet. I knew what it would take to get accepted to the Academy, and I vowed I wouldn't let anything get in my way."

Riker nodded. He knew what it took; he had put in years of preparation himself. But somehow there had been time for sports, for playing the piano, for reading. Even, in the crisp wilds of the snowy Alaskan forests, time just to walk and dream. Maybe that had been his mother's legacy: his father certainly never condoned giving time to daydreams.

"My parents were incredibly supportive," she went on. "The whole family was. My brother and my sister took over my chores so I'd have more time to study. Getting me into Starfleet was a family goal. They all sacrificed a lot to give me that chance, and I always felt I owed it to them to succeed."

She stirred vaguely at her salad. Riker found himself feeling sorry for her, this serious young woman with the overdeveloped sense of responsibility. He wondered if her family would enjoy knowing that she had given up everything in life that might be pleasurable except her work. Somehow he doubted it. They might be proud of her and gratified that the joint efforts had paid off; but surely they would want her to enjoy herself occasionally.

"Ensign, as your commanding officer, I have an order for you." Her head jerked up at this and she fixed him with a clear gaze.

"Yes, sir," she replied crisply. He almost smiled at her seriousness.

"I want you to find a hobby." She looked at him, perplexed. "Doesn't matter what, as long as you spend at least ten hours a week at it. And it *cannot* be work-related."

They were in the midst of discussing options, with Riker suggesting that he could teach her to play stand-up bass—she'd never *heard* of a stand-up bass

—when Dokachin sent a message from the surface informing them that he had found the collaborator.

The culprit was a female Zakdorn named Gelfina. She seemed pathetic to Riker, with her wrinkled, squat body and her whiny voice. She sat wringing her hands nervously, and her eyes were already wet. He felt that anything but a gentle approach would be brutal.

Gretchen felt no such compunctions.

To Riker's amazement, she was an intimidating interrogator, hammering away relentlessly, unmoved by the Zakdorn woman's tears and unswayed by her excuses.

"We've identified your computer-usage pattern," snapped Gretchen. "We've matched your personal and duty logs with the files documenting the transports to the *Tripoli*. If you believe we've made a mistake you'll be given the chance to make a typical entry so we can see if the same pattern occurs."

Gelfina shook her head miserably. She knew that usage patterns for a race as precise and meticulous as the Zakdorn were as identifiable as fingerprints are on humans. No two people used a computer in the same way, and the technology that could recognize the user through his or her pattern was well established.

"Then you acknowledge that we have correctly distinguished your signature?" Gretchen's voice was adamant, and Gelfina nodded, snuffling a bit as she did.

"Then you admit that you forged the locking coordinates of the *Tripoli* into the depot's computer system?"

The woman hesitated, looked around her, calculating her chances of getting out of this. Riker saw her give that up when she turned back to Gretchen, and looked into those green eyes, blazing now with intent. Gelfina nodded.

"Why?" asked Riker. He was always interested in what motivated people to act in ways that were ultimately against their own best interest. But this question only caused Gelfina to dissolve in tears—huge, wracking sobs that caused her pudgy shoulders to heave and shudder.

Gretchen shot him a look. She clearly felt the question and its resultant histrionics had gotten in the way of her clean drive toward the truth. And she was right. But Riker was still curious. Gelfina's sobs subsided and, for the first time, she spoke.

"He was nice to me," she burbled. "He said I was p-p-p-pretty," and then she dissolved once more in tears. Riker realized his curious question had unlocked more than motivation, and Gretchen realized the same. She flicked her eyes toward Gelfina and backed away. Riker moved forward and sat in front of the miserable Zakdorn woman.

"Gelfina," he said softly. "I know this is hard on you. But we need your help. I think someone has taken advantage of you. Can you tell me who it is?"

She wiped large hands across her porcine face, and struggled for control. "He didn't take advantage of me . . . he cared about me. He understood me. He was the only one who ever treated me that way . . . and now he's dead!" That brought on another episode of wailing, and Riker waited patiently until she could continue.

He reflected on the scenario that was unfolding. Gelfina, a squalid, torpid creature whose job as a computer technician was probably all she could ever look forward to, was easy prey for a seducer. A few soft words, a compliment, an understanding ear . . . and a grasping man could have just about anything he wanted.

"He was on the ship that exploded," Riker deduced, and Gelfina nodded, rubbing the backs of her hands across her eyes, which were now red and swollen. "What was his name?"

"M-M-Melcor." She shuddered, as though to say the name would undo her again.

"And he asked you to configure the computer system so everyone would think the *Tripoli* was still docked in its space?" Another nod. He sensed that Gelfina was becoming sullen again. "Do you know why he did it? What he did with the materiel he stole?"

An emphatic shake of the head.

"Do you know whom else he dealt with?" Another no. Riker leaned in close, and took her now wet hand in his. "Gelfina," he said gently, "you've been very brave. I'm going to recommend that the Zakdorn authorities treat you with understanding. But I would very much appreciate it if you could tell me the name of even one other person that Melcor knew."

At this her head snapped up and her round moon face took on a furious look. "Amarie," she snapped. "His fat, stupid, worthless, lazy, uncouth ex-wife."

Amarie sucked a salt stick with one hand as she played the keyboard with the other three. She'd been swearing she'd give them up for months, and once she'd gone as long as four days without one. But the cravings became so intense that she found herself holding a stick with trembling fingers, licking it desperately, without remembering any conscious decision to do so.

After that, she gave up. What the rune, anyway? So she lived a few months less. The way her life was going she wouldn't miss those months, and maybe be glad to check out sooner rather than later.

Amarie sighed and put down the salt stick, joined her fourth hand to the keyboard. This was what the customers at Shern's Palace came to hear: all four hands blazing away on the keys and Amarie's ample girth jiggling to the beat of her music. Although, as she looked around, she realized not many *were* coming anymore. The bar was nearly empty; only a few jaded regulars sat at tables and mostly they ignored her music.

Who could blame them? They'd heard it all before. There were no new customers; the only ones who came here any more were those with nowhere else to go. Shern's Palace, indeed. Some palace. It was a tacky, overblown hideaway that had already seen its glory days. The decor was pure Zakdorn, even though Shern was a Filimase: lots of red panels, with ropes and nets and chains and—did *anyone* still do those? —stone *shriva* birds at the entrance.

Amarie had long since found she could do an evening's set at the keys without her mind ever being engaged in the music. It was rote to her by now, her repertoire so extensive that she could segue from piece to piece without having to direct her conscious mind to the process.

Unfortunately, that gave her a lot of time to think. Thinking wasn't something she enjoyed much these days; too much in her life was disappointing. All the wrong turns and bad choices kept recycling in her mind like a feedback loop. Mostly those choices involved men, rune them. Frank, Nard, Melcor, Renninum . . . losers every one. What was it about her that kept attracting this space flotsam? Weren't there any good men left in the galaxy?

She glanced over toward a wall panel where she knew she could catch her reflection, and grabbed a few licks of salt as she did. She looked good enough, she thought. Maybe she was a little heavier than when she was young, but roundness was not necessarily a drawback; lots of men liked a little bounce in a woman, and Amarie could bounce with the best. Her hair was always neatly done, its black ringlets upswept, and her makeup artfully applied—quickly, too, because her four arms came in handy for more than keyboard playing (and more than a few men would agree with her). Her nose rings were elaborate and artfully inserted; her gown was one of her best—a rose color (quite flattering to her), with just a bit of a sheen to it.

"Amarie, my pumply . . ." The dreaded voice of Shern, the owner of the hideaway, knifed into her reverie. She glanced up at him with a bored expression.

"What, Shern?"

"The patrons they are asleep falling. May we not more music lively be having?"

Shern drove her crazy. In this age of the Universal Translator, there was simply no reason not to use one. Why Shern had to murder the language in his pathetic attempts to be native was beyond her. She hated his thin, scaly face and his unblinking, beady eye. But mostly she loathed him because he held her livelihood in his control, and lately it seemed she could not please him, no matter what. Well, rune him.

"I do my kind of music, Shern. You liked it when you hired me."

"But the sameness again and again occurs. Is not there some variety possible being?"

Variety. She could play maybe four thousand separate melodies, enough to run continuously for several days, and he accused her of not having variety. Annoyed, she grabbed at her salt stick and stuck it in her mouth. "You tell me what you want, Shern, I'll give it to you. Better than anybody else you could get to do this job for what you're paying." The words were a little muffled behind the salt, but she knew he'd get the idea.

"If no there is customers more, job will be continuing not," he hissed, and, glowering at her portentously, moved off.

Amarie's second-greatest fear was that she would spend out her days in this runey little hovel, sucking salt and making music, without ever knowing the love of a good man or the fulfillment of children.

Her greatest fear was that she would *not* spend out her days here, would in fact not spend any more of them here, and be cast out jobless to make her way on Qualor in whatever fashion she could work out. And that would be next to impossible, because she and the weird little runes known as Zakdorn did not get along at all.

She'd never have chosen this place to live; it was light-years from her home planet in more ways than distance. Talemstra, where she'd been born, was inhabited by a peace-loving, creative species, all of whom had four arms and who used them in the pursuit of the arts. Music, sculpture, dance—her people delighted in these activities, and Amarie would give anything if she could get back to them. She'd been abandoned on Zakdorn by her third husband, Nard, a handsome adventurer who had his own starship, but who unfortunately also had a roving eye. He'd left her for a Siblite beauty who was too young for him, and far too thin, and she figured they hadn't lasted long at all. But in the meantime, she was stuck on Zakdorn.

She hated it here. They were such dull, officious little runes; they had no appreciation for a creative soul. And she was incapable of doing any of the jobs they offered her—she couldn't deal with columns of numbers and lists of files. Music was all she knew, and if she lost this job she'd be in real trouble. She'd die homeless and friendless on this awful planet, with no one to mourn her passing.

Amarie crunched the last of her salt stick in her mouth and winced as the bitter granules went down her throat. She took one hand to wash it down with Trastor ale, then attacked the keyboard with all four hands. She'd make Shern eat his words. Variety? She'd show him variety.

She was working the quartet of arms into a lather when she saw the man walk in, and her heart suddenly pounded. He was tall and breathtakingly handsome, with a neatly trimmed beard and mustache. He was dressed in a well-tailored red outfit—a uniform?— and he had eyes the color of the seas on Hoalot.

There was a woman with him, and she was thin— planklike actually. Amarie knew that kind of skin-and-bones could never bounce a man like this. The woman's hair was dark and neatly tied, her face

looked drab without makeup, and she wore the same
outfit as the man, only it was a brownish color.

Amarie intensified the beat of the music and swayed
on her stool. She'd get that man up here and they'd
make real music together.

For the first time that night, Amarie smiled.

Riker's eyes swept the murky interior of the hideaway. There were few patrons; those that were there
tended to hover in the shadows toward the rear. What
were clearly prostitutes lounged in a bored fashion
along the bar, but there were no takers.

He was aware of Gretchen at his side, studying the
room as intently as he; he wondered if he'd been wise
in bringing her. She'd been determined to come, of
course, and Worf had backed her up: the Klingon
lieutenant liked to know that one of his trained people
was along on any away mission.

Nonetheless, this sordid little den was not, in
Riker's mind, the place for a young woman from
Indiana. He knew Gretchen would be furious if she
knew he was thinking that, and he would never voice
it aloud; but call him old-fashioned, this was no place
for a lady.

He'd spotted Amarie the moment they came in; she
was notable because of her four arms, but even
without those he'd have recognized her. She was
blowsy and plump, with frizzy dyed black hair and too
much makeup; cheap-looking artificial jewelry
adorned her fingers, her hair, and her nose. Her pink
sequined gown was loose and flowing, but it did not
conceal her ample girth.

"Take a seat here, I'll be back in a while." Riker

gestured toward a small table and saw Gretchen's predictable reaction—her eyes widened in surprise and then narrowed in resistance.

"I think I should stay with you, Commander," she said quietly. "After all, I am assigned to you as security."

He smiled easily. "Understood, Ensign. But I have sized up the situation and examined the objective. And I promise you this is one case where I will function better on my own."

Her eyes blinked and he pulled out a chair for her. "I'd suggest you stick to the Trastor ale. It's tasty, and it won't put you on your ear like some other drinks they probably serve here." There was a brief moment, and then Gretchen sat, though reluctantly.

"All right, Commander," she said. "But I'll be watching."

"I hope so. That's your job." And he smiled down at her.

He felt, rather than heard, the music take a jump in energy, and glanced up toward the spotlighted center of the room where Amarie sat at the keyboard. Briefly touching Gretchen on the shoulder, he moved toward the light.

The woman was sucking on a salt stick as she played, seemingly oblivious to his approach, though Riker's instincts told him she was very aware. He sat at one of the unoccupied stools that surrounded the keyboard instrument. Amarie gave him a quick, non-committal glance.

"A new face," she drawled in a husky voice.

"Same one I've always had," countered Riker, and was pleased to see a ready grin spread her lips. He liked people with humor; it made everything so much easier.

"What would you like to hear?" she asked, fingers roaming the keys. Riker was fascinated by the rippling counterpoints she could produce with her four hands.

"Know the blues?" he asked.

Another grin on her generous mouth. "Look at me, mister. What do you think?"

Riker decided he liked this woman. She was garish, but at the core she was earthy and honest. "Seven different shades of them," she continued. "How about some low-down Andorian blues?"

Two hands shifted into a bluesy riff, another worked the salt stick, and the fourth offered him one from a nearby bowl. "Suck salt?" she queried.

"Never cared for it," replied Riker. He thought it a disgusting habit, and wondered if the people who were caught up in it realized what it did to their mouths. He'd dated a woman once who loved her salt sticks, and every time he kissed her he felt his own mouth pucker and dry; it was like kissing a desert floor.

"Good for you. Nasty habit." She took a few more licks and then put the stick down. Without looking at him, she said, "Who are you looking for?"

Caught a little off-guard, Riker felt his reply was bumbling. "Who says I'm looking for anybody?"

"Your face. Your uniform. In a place like this."

"Okay. I'm looking for you."

"You just made my day." Amarie's delivery was dry, but Riker felt there was a truth in the words that she would never admit to.

"I have to ask you about your husband."

Amarie cast him a glance and her music took on a

different tone—a little busier, more urgent. "Well, it was nice while it lasted," she said with studied nonchalance. "Which husband?"

"The dead one, I'm afraid."

She kept playing, never missing a beat. But that faintly frantic element was still in the music. "You must be from the *Enterprise,*" she said laconically. "You destroyed his ship."

Riker was relieved that she wasn't a game player. This whole endeavor could have been protracted interminably, but Amarie was not a guileful woman. He wondered what feelings she might still have for the dead man who piloted the smuggler's ship, so he trod carefully. With a touch of regret in his voice, he said, "He fired first."

"He always did." Riker gave her a sharp glance, looking for any hidden meaning, but her face was neutral.

"He was involved in some pretty bad business," he continued. "And he took the evidence with him."

"His one endearing quality—he always cleaned up after himself." Now Riker thought he saw a twinkle in her eye. "What do you want from me?" she asked.

"I was hoping you might know his business partners."

Amarie sighed faintly and looked down at her hands, moving idly over the keys. "Why should I help you?" she asked softly.

"To be honest, I can't think of a good reason." He smiled at her, and hoped honesty appealed to an honest woman.

"Well, you did kill my ex-husband. That's not a bad start." He shook his head, grinning at her; the more he sat here, the more he liked her. "Why don't you drop a few coins in the jar," she suggested. "I'll see what I remember."

"I don't carry money," he said truthfully. She gave him an appraising glance, and then sighed again.

"You don't offer much, do you?"

Riker considered this. It was true. He was asking for information—a commodity of great value to him. And he had nothing to offer in return. There was something unfair about it. What might this used-up woman want, he wondered, except a man to treat her decently and take her away from all this?

Then it occurred to him what it might be.

"Slide over," he ordered.

She looked at him in surprise. "What?"

Riker got up and sat next to her at the piano, catching a whiff of her salty breath. He reached toward the keys.

"Just what I need—another set of hands," she commented.

"You know this one?" He began to play the way he had in the re-creation of Stumpy's place on the holodeck. "Early twentieth century, from a place on Earth called Memphis." He played for a moment and could tell from her reaction that she was responding. "Maybe," he suggested, "I could teach you a lick or two."

"You already have," she acknowledged, watching his hands carefully, absorbing the riffs, studying the way his fingers drifted over the keys. She was genuinely impressed, loving the music, moved by its heartfelt origins.

He played for a few moments, and then ventured idly, "So, what do you say?"

She shrugged, looked up at him, gave him that ready grin. "Gonna be around a few days?"

"I can be."

"Sooner or later, a man named Omag will come by for a song. Always wants to hear the same thing—'Melor Famagal.' He's an arms trader. A fat Ferengi."

Riker stared at her. This was it, the connection he'd been looking for. The sensation of victory welled up in him and he laid into the keys, pulling the music up from some place deep within. At some point he realized Amarie's four hands had joined his, and they continued to make sweet six-handed blues for a long time.

Chapter Fourteen

SPOCK SAT WITH Pardek in the outer chamber of Proconsul Neral's suite of offices. They had climbed through the grandiose chambers of the nearly kilometer-high governmental edifice, the Irnilt, and Spock had noted the statelines of the architecture, the clean elegance of the design. The rooms were vaulted and spacious, and conveyed an impression of urbanity and power. The grandeur of the building was in marked contrast to the rough streets of the city, the fetid passageways where people lived in abject desolation. The contrast was fascinating.

He had become aware, as they made their way through the building, that Pardek was a man whose time of power was waning. Pardek smiled and called out to everyone they met, and the replies were always gracious. But he was certain that Pardek was the needy part of the equation; those who possessed power did not need to seek so blatantly the recognition of others. That did not concern Spock. Pardek's value was to initiate the meeting for which they had climbed the imposing black marble stairs of the Irnilt.

Now, waiting in the outer chamber for Neral to receive them, Spock observed Pardek chatting amiably with a woman who had introduced herself as an associate to Neral. She was, Spock noted, an unusual-looking Romulan, in that her hair was blond. Pardek was avuncular and friendly to her, but Spock sensed that even she kept herself at a remove from him, and was talking out of courtesy rather than choice.

It was not a good sign that they were being kept waiting. If this meeting were in fact the priority that Pardek insisted it was, they would not be kept on this hard bench in the lobby to make conversation with functionaries. For a brief moment the echo of Sarek's —Picard's?—skepticism resonated in his mind.

Spock was relieved when a young man came scurrying from Neral's office and announced that the proconsul would now see them. Pardek broke off his conversation with the assistant and hurried over to Spock, his round, friendly face beaming with happiness.

"Shall we?" he asked, and Spock rose to follow him inside the inner chamber.

The man who greeted them was younger than Spock had imagined. He had heard the proconsul described as a youthful, dynamic leader, but this man seemed almost boyish. His eyes were dark and flashing, and his smile was immediate. He moved across the room toward them, his step buoyant.

"Proconsul." Pardek's voice was a bit ingratiating.

"Yes . . . Pardek . . . come in," said Neral. But his eyes were on Spock.

"Ambassador Spock of Vulcan," said Pardek unnecessarily.

"Proconsul," said Spock evenly. He held Neral's look.

"Please," said Neral, waving the appellation away. "I've never liked titles since I was a lowly Uhlan in the Romulan guard. I am Neral." He lifted his hand, looked at it in comic uncertainty. "Now, how is it again? Pardek's tried to show me . . ."

He finally managed to arrange his fingers in the Vulcan greeting. Spock returned it. "I am honored," he said.

"Good," replied Neral. The two men held a look once again.

Pardek smiled nervously and Spock knew he felt like the outsider here in his own country's seat of power. "Permit me to withdraw," he said, and Spock caught the touch of obsequiousness in his voice.

Neral turned to Pardek with practiced diplomacy. "Will we see you and your wife tomorrow at the state dinner?"

Pardek beamed with pleasure. "We're looking forward to it," he said, and bowed his head slightly. He turned and exited.

Neral turned back to Spock; the inflection of his voice implied that they shared some commonalty as he said, "It's been years since old Pardek was invited to an official function. He's far too attached to the common man for most people's comfort."

"That is their loss," replied Spock. He would not be disloyal to Pardek now, after all these years. "I've always found Pardek to have a unique insight into many issues."

Neral didn't respond, but waved him into a comfortable chair covered in some kind of softly tooled hide. "Let me tell you something, Spock," he said without preamble. "We're going to start something here, you and I, that will redraw the face of the quadrant."

Spock was startled. He had been prepared to speak eloquently about his cause, had hoped to persuade— but had not expected to hear Neral already committed. Perhaps he was reading more into the proconsul's statement than was intended. "You are prepared to support reunification?" he asked, wanting clarification.

"I believe it must eventually come. Our two worlds need each other."

"Forgive me. But I did not expect to hear a Romulan proconsul speak like a member of the underground."

Neral smiled comfortably. "I want you to know exactly where I stand."

Spock pondered this unusual turn for a long moment. It was an unexpected gift that Neral seemed predisposed to unification. But then, he was part of a young, liberal generation of leaders; if he in fact represented the future, there was reason for hope. On the other hand, the proconsul's views were not necessarily those of the rest of the leadership. "Do you believe you can gain the support of the full Senate?" asked Spock.

Neral leaned in to him, speaking not conspiratorially, but with a quiet confidence. "Things are not what they once were in the Senate. The old leaders have lost the respect of the people." He stood and began to pace. "Involvement in the Klingon civil war . . . endless confrontations with the Federation . . . The people are tired of it all. Times are changing. Leaders who refuse to change with them—will no longer be leaders."

He turned back to Spock, enthusiasm apparent in every aspect. "Spock, I am prepared to *publicly* endorse the opening of talks between our peoples." He smiled at Spock's obvious astonishment. "How do you think the Vulcan people will respond to that?"

Spock did not hasten to reply. Things were moving quickly; he preferred to keep his own measured pace. He had found over a lifetime that haste was rarely an ally. Finally he said, "They will be cautious. There are generations of distrust to overcome."

Neral was obviously perplexed by his cautious reply. "But surely," he began, "with a man of your influence leading the way—"

Then a disembodied voice on the Romulan comm system interrupted. "Proconsul," announced the associate from her outer chamber, "the Senate has been recalled into session."

Neral frowned briefly, then replied, "Very well." He turned to Spock. "Can we meet again tomorrow?"

"As you wish," offered Spock phlegmatically.

"Good," replied Neral. *"Jolan tru,* Spock." Then, remembering something, he added, "Oh—live long and prosper."

Spock bowed gravely and exited. He was left with a distinct feeling: the conversation was not logical.

D'Tan had been running for over an hour. He had at least another hour to go, but he knew he could keep his pace easily. In fact, he could probably go on indefinitely. There was something glorious about the feel of the wind on his face and the thud of his feet on the hot Romulan clay as he loped through the Valley of Chula. D'Tan never felt as good as he did when he was running.

Everyone was always telling him to slow down, but he never did. Why slow down? There was so much to do, to know, to learn. He was often afraid that he would die without having tasted all that life had to offer, and he didn't want to waste precious minutes by strolling. So he ran.

Eventually those who had admonished him to slow down began to realize that his running was of value. The movement had begun using him as a messenger, for he was more trustworthy than any other means of communication; and to the followers of the movement, trust was a more important property than speed.

He was running now toward an outlying community, M'Narth, carrying an important message. There was to be a meeting tonight in the caves and everyone must be there. It might be the most important meeting they'd ever held.

That was the sum total of the message; D'Tan had been told nothing more. But in his heart he felt that the realization of their dream was near. Spock would be giving them the news they were all waiting to hear: that they would be joining with their Vulcan cousins once more.

For D'Tan and his family, and for many of their friends, it was a dream that had been carefully preserved for generations. D'Tan had been raised, as his parents had been raised, and their parents before them and back and back for many generations, with the belief that someday the Vulcan and the Romulan races would be reunited. That a day of harmony and peace would arrive in which all of them would mingle together, without barriers and without prejudice.

The first songs D'Tan had heard as an infant were Vulcan songs; the first stories his mother told him were stories of Vulcan. He had been steeped in Vulcan lore and Vulcan history. The desire to see this legendary planet and to live in meditative serenity with his brothers was a burning passion, and the thought that it might happen in his lifetime was exhilarating.

It was Spock who made the difference. Spock! The name rang on his tongue like a chime, and D'Tan found himself singing one of the unification songs, inserting Spock's name for that of an ancient hero. Singing made the time pass more quickly, and he wanted the hours until the meeting tonight to flash by as quickly as possible.

That night, in the caves, D'Tan's heart was pounding and his face was flushed with excitement. He could hardly believe what he was hearing, and he knew everyone in the cavernous meeting place felt the same. They were hushed; no one stirred, not even the small children, who seemed to understand that this was an important occasion. Spock's calm voice echoed through the chamber, describing in detail his meeting that very day with Neral, making it clear that the proconsul was receptive to him and apparently to his ideas.

Somewhere in the crowd a baby began to cry; soft sucking sounds told D'Tan that it was quickly silenced at its mother's breast. And then Spock made the most incredible statement of all: the proconsul endorsed unification and was willing to make a public statement urging talks between Romulan and Vulcan leaders!

A huge cry of joy rang out in the caves; neighbor embraced neighbor and people babbled excitedly over the unexpected news. D'Tan's father held him tightly in an embrace and his mother held both his hands in hers. His friend Janicka, who sat nearby, was crying with joy. D'Tan thought he had never been so happy in his life.

"A public statement . . ."

"We will live with our cousins . . ."

"No more hiding in caves . . ."

The people were overjoyed. A young woman named Shalote, unable to contain her elation, jumped to her feet and took Spock's hand, pressing it in gratitude. "It's everything we could have hoped for," she cried, and the crowd clamored its agreement.

Why, then, that frown on Spock's face? Why did he turn to survey the euphoric crowd with such a glowering look? Suddenly D'Tan was frightened.

Spock's voice rang out over the rejoicing. "It is *more* than we could have hoped for," he announced.

And a startled hush fell over the group. D'Tan saw Pardek register the same confusion as the crowd.

"But if Neral is ready to publicly endorse reunification . . ." began the good senator, then left the sentence unfinished, staring at Spock in bewilderment.

Only one man seemed even to understand what Spock was saying, and that was the captain from the Federation, Picard. D'Tan swallowed, not sure he wanted to hear what was coming next.

"I can't imagine that one rises to the position of

Senate proconsul without the support of the Romulan traditionalists," began Picard, directing the statement to Pardek.

"That's true," replied the senator.

The Federation man seemed to bore into Pardek. "Then how can he turn his back on them so easily? How can he endorse reunification when it is considered *subversive?*"

A man from the crowd stepped forward and interjected. "Because he's not afraid of them. Because he knows we will support him!" Even to D'Tan, the man sounded desperate.

Spock's composed voice rang through the cavern. "Captain Picard is correct. It is not logical for the proconsul to endorse reunification at this time."

And now the crowd erupted, clamoring their objections. D'Tan heard his own voice among them, and felt his eyes sting with tears of frustration. How could Spock do this? Could he not see that their dreams, their prayers, were just on the verge of being answered? Was he being swayed by the Starfleet captain who had arrived so unexpectedly? Was he to snatch this bright promise from them when it meant so much?

Shalote was trembling with anger. "Why would Neral lie?" she demanded.

"Perhaps they are hoping to use this to expose members of your movement," Picard answered, and D'Tan saw the woman flash him a bitter look.

"No," she cried out, "this is our chance for acceptance. Finally, to be heard!"

Another man from the crowd joined in. "I believe it is the *Federation* that fears an alliance between Romulus and Vulcan!"

Now the crowd's rumble took an ugly turn, and D'Tan felt its wrath as though it were a living animal, coiling and writhing, turning to cast its eye on Picard. The outsider. The interloper. One on whom they could vent their anger and disappointment.

The clamor grew louder and more menacing. Picard faced them, and D'Tan sensed no fear in him, but rather a desire to quell the gathering fury of the mob. "That is not true—" he began, but he was shouted down.

Then Spock stepped forward, his look enough to quiet the unruliest of throngs. He stared at the seething mass of humanity, silent until they withered under his gaze and settled into a restive, murmuring mass.

"I came here," said Spock quietly, and by his hushed tone silenced the crowd further, "to determine the potential for reunification. In spite of what has occurred, I intend to continue my efforts. I intend to meet with the proconsul as planned."

A huge roar of approval thundered through the caves. Instantly the mood of the people had turned once more to joyous approbation.

D'Tan thought he might have been the only person in the cave who saw the look that passed between Spock and Picard. To him, it seemed charged with conflict. Then Spock turned and left the main chamber, and after a moment, Picard followed him.

D'Tan felt that the destiny of his people walked with those two men at that moment.

As Picard followed Spock down the narrow passageway into the small, damp chamber adjoining the large cavern, he was smoldering with anger. He would never have thought that Spock could be swayed by a surly crowd, but he had just seen it happen. Some part of his mind realized that he felt personally betrayed by the ambassador's actions, and that thought puzzled him for a moment—why personally?—but then his ire pushed it from his consciousness.

Ahead, Spock turned to face him. Picard perceived suddenly that Spock had not come here to confer with him, but to be alone, and was not pleased to find Picard dogging his heels. He didn't care; Spock would have to deal with him.

"You let their emotions sway you," he charged, hoping Spock would answer in angry kind.

But of course he did not. Spock raised an eyebrow and intoned in a slightly surprised fashion, "On the contrary, I am pursuing the most logical course."

Picard took a breath and tried to calm himself. It would serve nothing to run at this man in a white heat. "You are as skeptical as I am," he said, looking for the argument that would appeal to reason. "Is it logical to ignore your own good sense?"

"I fear the influence of Sarek has colored your attitudes, Captain. Toward reunification. And perhaps toward me."

Picard was taken aback. How did Sarek become a participant in this interpersonal drama? His mind flashed back to the discussion he and Spock had had in the soup stall. Spock had accused him of having a closed mind . . . and at the time Picard had been puzzled. It was as though Spock were accusing him of having another man's feelings. And now, here it was again.

"This is the second time you have accused me of speaking with another man's voice," he said carefully, watching for Spock's reaction. The Vulcan gazed at him without expression, but Picard sensed a maelstrom of feeling behind his eyes. He knew it was time to acknowledge Sarek's influence. "Yes, he will always be a part of me. His experiences. His spirit. But I speak with my own voice, Spock. Not his."

There was a long moment. Picard heard the dripping of the moisture on the walls, the rush of distant underground waters. The face of his own father flashed briefly in his mind.

And finally, Spock drew a breath. "Curious," he said, "that I should hear him so clearly . . . now that he is dead."

The Vulcan moved away then, and Picard recognized the movement as an effort to regain emotional control. "It is possible," he said evenly, "that I have brought my arguments with Sarek to you, Captain. If so, I apologize."

"Is it so important," said Picard softly, "for you to win one last argument with him?"

Spock considered the statement as though he were pondering the hypothetical premise of a scientific inquiry. "No," he said solemnly, "it is not."

Then he turned, and with a naked honesty that caught Picard like the chill gust of a winter breeze, said, "Although it is true that I will miss the arguments. It was, finally, all that we had."

With startling clarity, Picard understood. In some unspoken fashion, he had become father to Spock— Spock, almost a century older than he. The mind meld with Sarek had blended them in some indescribable fashion. To what extent he *was* Sarek, and to what extent Spock simply *heard* Sarek, he did not know. But he knew that in a strange, unbidden way he had indeed done what Sarek had asked of him; he had come to Romulus and allowed that relationship to play out its final hand.

Perhaps he could effect closure between the father and the son. Perhaps he could grant absolution. Perhaps he could speak the words that Sarek never would.

"Your fight with Sarek is over," he said with simple sincerity. "And you have none with me."

Spock turned away, and Picard sensed his Vulcan desire to place this discussion in a rational context. But what he heard was a son struggling to achieve the termination of a protracted and difficult relationship —and not succeeding.

"I always had a different vision from my father's," he said. "It was an ability to see *beyond* pure logic. He considered it weak. But I have discovered it to be a source of extraordinary strength."

Picard questioned the reasoning of this statement. If anything, Sarek had always been more emotional than Spock. Spock's decision to follow Vulcan, rather than human, behavior had caused him to eschew emotions and to deify reason. But he realized that what Spock was uttering was not reality, but rather his perception of reality—his feelings. Picard did not comment.

"Sarek would find this mission of reunification a fool's errand," Spock continued, turning the conversation back to the case at hand. "But somehow I think it is not. Logic cannot explain why . . . but I know I must continue to pursue this—"

"Even," Picard now interjected, "if it leads you into a Romulan trap?"

Spock shrugged. "If the Romulans do have an

ulterior motive, it would be in the interests of all concerned to determine what it is."

And for that, Picard had no answer.

"So I will play the role they would have me play," Spock summed up, and Picard could only acknowledge reluctantly the rightness of his instincts.

Chapter Fifteen

CAPTAIN K'VADA had been sure he would not scream when his shoulder was dislocated by the ship's physician. He had anticipated the pain, explored it in his mind, and prepared his defenses. When K'kam had torn it from its socket the first time, the wound was unexpected, and he felt justified in having uttered a brief howl at the agony of his arm being wrenched from its joint.

He had not lost consciousness. He had not thrown up. He had not uttered a cry beyond that first roar. It was a response to injury that would make any Klingon proud.

And so he was sure that this second violation of his tortured shoulder was within his control.

Sitting in the small, dark cubicle assigned to the ship's physician, K'Vada listened to Klarg, the doctor. Klarg was a heavy, blowsy man of indeterminate age who wheezed as he talked. The physician had convinced K'Vada that the incessant pain he felt was due to an incorrect alignment of the shoulder in its socket. The only remedy was to pull the ball of the shoulder from its joint and then reinsert it properly.

K'Vada knew that scar tissue would have developed around the injury. He knew that this tissue would have to be ripped in order to reposition the bone.

What he hadn't realized was how excruciating that process would be.

Klarg was to blame for it, he was sure. Had the Klingon doctor not been inept and doddering, the pain would have been manageable. But the idiot, instead of quickly snapping the shoulder loose, pried and twisted as though he were *trying* to torture K'Vada. It went on interminably, and though he dug his nails into his palms until they bled, and finally bit into his tongue in a desperate effort to create pain somewhere else besides his shoulder, the cry escaped his lips.

He had thought it was just a strangled moan, but from the startled look on Klarg's face, it must have been far more—a shriek, a humiliating admission of weakness. With his newly dislocated arm dangling at his side, he kicked the doctor across the room.

That had perhaps been a bad decision.

Klarg was dazed and injured. K'Vada could see that he was stumbling as he made his way back across the room. He was not a young man, and unaccustomed to physicality.

"Replace my arm!" K'Vada yelled at him. He had not undergone this much suffering to be left with a useless appendage.

Klarg looked up at him, his bony brow distended, his eyes bugged in a strange and disturbing way. He was gasping for breath and his face was seeping fluids. K'Vada stared at him. Was the *patahk* going to die? Without having relocated his shoulder socket?

K'Vada had a moment of panic, and tried to lift the doctor from his kneeling position. "Get up," he commanded. "Do your duty to me!"

But Klarg slumped against him, driving a new shot of pain into his arm. To his horror, the ship's physician passed out and his breathing became reedy and shallow. He *was* going to die.

K'Vada glared at him. For a moment he *hoped* Klarg would die, as punishment for putting him in this dreadful predicament. Then he had a moment of panic as he realized that, with Klarg dead, no one on board could properly reposition his arm, and he would more than likely be permanently disfigured.

He considered trying to reinsert the arm himself. A warrior, on the field of battle, might be faced with such a challenge. Would Kahless have quailed at the thought of pain? Would he have despaired of preserving consciousness while twisting his bones through ripped tendons and into their proper resting place? Never.

Klarg turned gray at his feet, gasping noisily, as K'Vada stood, trying to convince himself to take hold of his useless arm and force it into its resting place.

Finally, it occurred to K'Vada that he really should see to Klarg before he took any drastic action with his arm, and he bellowed for help. Scurrying minions arrived and he ordered attention to Klarg, all the while concealing from them his damaged arm.

He made his way to the bridge, still uncertain as to what his next action should be. He searched his memory for anyone on board who possessed rudimentary medical skills, and could think of no one. He fought panic. On a Klingon ship, the weak were expendable. It was a mark of honor to assassinate one's superior; if someone were weak and careless enough to be taken in such a fashion, he did not deserve either to lead or to live.

K'Vada would be dead within days if it were learned that he was defenseless. And it wouldn't take long before someone would notice that he couldn't even lift his arm, much less defend himself with it.

He considered ordering an aide to hack it off at the shoulder; such a dismemberment, if it were borne stoically, brought honor. Men often lost limbs in battle, and proudly waved their stumps as badges of courage. He might even be able to concoct a plausible tale to explain the loss of his arm, one which would bring him glory. He mused briefly about this possibility, imagined the bite of the sword into his shoulder, anticipated the sound and the smell as a torch cauterized the wound. The thought made him dizzy, and as he entered the bridge he had to will himself to walk purposefully past the crew, being careful not to grimace from the pain each step caused.

He was sitting in his command chair, fighting waves of nausea, when the android Data entered the bridge and went directly to a computer station.

"What are you after now?" K'Vada growled, and he heard the sound of pain in his own voice.

The Starfleet officer turned, but K'Vada couldn't tell if he heard it, too. "I am attempting to penetrate the Romulan data network. It is protected by sophisticated security measures."

"You have a console in your quarters," snapped K'Vada, irritated to have this stranger on his bridge now, of all times.

"I am sorry if I am intruding," replied Data. "You had given your permission for me to use the more powerful computer array on the bridge in order to access the Romulan data banks."

It was true, he had. It seemed light-years ago that he had dreamt of honor and accolades for accessing Romulan intelligence nets. All that mattered now was ridding himself of the excruciating pain that riddled his body and was beginning to make his vision bleary.

K'Vada blinked through sweat and suddenly saw the android's pale face just inches from his. He was expressing concern, saying—what? K'Vada squeezed his eyes shut and forced himself to stay conscious.

". . . seem to be in some distress . . ." he heard Data saying. "Perhaps I could be of help." The android was offering to help him. How could he possibly—

"My arm . . ." breathed K'Vada, desperate as a child.

And Data was gently inspecting his arm and shoulder, his synthetic touch strangely painless. "With your permission, sir?" he asked, and when K'Vada merely nodded grimly, a sudden, simple motion and K'Vada's arm was resting in its socket, neatly housed, in its correct position, he could tell—the pain still there but somehow dwindling to a tolerable ache.

He tested the motion gingerly. He could lift his arm—not to full height, but the range of motion was surprisingly complete. The pain was receding rapidly.

"I have a hypospray I could apply that would reduce swelling and aid in the healing of the ligaments," Data was saying. And K'Vada could only nod numbly, more grateful than he would ever be able to admit. The android left the bridge to get his medicaments, and K'Vada felt an unaccustomed stinging in his eye; a wetness formed.

His arm would heal. He would be a warrior once more, claiming honor on the battlefield and acclaim among his fellows. He would lift the *bat'telh* in victory, its curved blade streaming blood, and taste the sweet mysteries of conquest and death.

And when, steaming and elated, he confronted K'kam, he would clasp her to him with two strong arms, holding her fury contained until, under his expert ministrations, she erupted in cataclysmic pleasure.

He almost wept with gratitude to the android.

When Spock and Picard transported back to the *Kruge,* it was in silence. Their discussion in the caves had left Spock with much to ponder, and he assumed from Picard's quiet introspection that the same was true of the captain.

Nonetheless, he had been intrigued when Picard mentioned the android's attempt to penetrate the Romulan data banks. This was an audacious endeavor, and perhaps doomed to failure, but Spock knew that its success would probably answer his most deep-seated questions about the Romulan mission.

And so he was curious to see what progress Commander Data had made. When the doors opened to his and Picard's quarters, Spock was not focused on the surroundings, but when he entered, they demanded his attention.

He was astonished at the small, spare quarters. He

had crossed the Neutral Zone in a Barolian freighter, and his accommodations were better than this. He cast a surprised glance at Picard, but the captain had clearly gotten beyond his environment sometime ago and now took it for granted.

"Have you had any success, Mr. Data?" Picard queried.

"Negative, Captain. The Romulan information net employs a progressive encryption lock. I have been unable to penetrate their security measures."

"May I assist you, Commander?" asked Spock. "I've had some experience in these matters." Spock realized that he was looking forward to this technological challenge.

"By all means, Ambassador," replied Data, and Spock moved to sit next to him. He was instantly absorbed in the problem.

"The Romulans have incorporated a forty-three-part cipher key into their entry sequence," said Spock, knowing that Data had covered this material.

"Yes, sir. The twenty-ninth is the only one I cannot bypass," Data responded.

Spock was vaguely aware that Picard was still in the room, and apparently feeling superfluous. "I think I'll take this opportunity to remove my ears," the Captain said, and exited.

Spock was glad he was gone. He remembered distantly that one frequently accomplished more when one's captain was out of the picture. And he had been looking forward to the opportunity to discuss Picard with his second.

"He intrigues me, this Picard," he said.

Data was instantly curious. "In what manner?" he asked.

"He is remarkably analytical and dispassionate for a human. I understand why my father would choose to mind meld with him. There's almost a Vulcan quality to the man."

"Interesting," responded Data. "I have never considered that. And Captain Picard has been a role model in my quest to be more human."

This took Spock aback. "To be *more* human?"

"Yes, Ambassador."

Spock raised an eyebrow. "Fascinating," he murmured. "You have an efficient intellect, superior physical skills, and no emotional impediments. There are Vulcans who aspire all their lives to achieve what you were given by design."

Spock could see the android processing this statement. He was silent for a moment, and then turned back to Spock.

"You are half human."

"Yes."

"And yet you have chosen a Vulcan way of life."

"I have."

"In effect, you have abandoned what I have sought all my life."

This innocent remark struck a surprisingly strong chord in Spock. His choice, as a child, to follow the Vulcan ways and eschew emotions had not been lightly made. It had required a lifetime of discipline and meditation in order to repress the human side of him. He was not sure he wanted to consider an inquiry into what he might have lost by the process.

He took refuge in the monitor before him. "I believe I have isolated the twenty-ninth cipher access code. I'll attempt to access the proconsul's files." He skillfully worked the controls of the computer, looking for paths into the files.

"Ambassador, may I ask a personal question?" Data's voice was infinitely polite.

"Please."

"As you examine your life, do you find you have missed your humanity?"

The computer made a series of beeps and Spock took advantage of this activity to organize his thoughts. That the android had seemingly tapped into his thoughts was uncanny. He considered his answer carefully. Finally, casually, he said, "I have no regrets," and continued to work on accessing the files.

"'No regrets.' That is a human expression," observed Data.

Spock was silent for a time. Then he said, "Fascinating."

Chapter Sixteen

AMARIE PICKED AT a rough spot in her fingernail until it became a gouge. Then she picked at it with another hand. She was trying not to hear what Shern was saying to her.

They were sitting in Shern's tiny little cubicle of an office at the rear of the hideaway, where he had summoned her for this impromptu "conference." Amarie hated his office. It was decorated with Shern's usual tacky taste: lots of red, chains piled on the floor, nets over the windows. Shern was so predictable.

Now, as his voice droned on and on, she looked down at the afflicted fingernail, concentrating on it with fierce intensity, as though it were the most important thing in the galaxy at that moment.

I'll have to redo the polish before tonight, she thought, dimly aware that Shern's voice continued to rasp in her ears. She tried not to look at his smooth, bloodless face, or that unblinking eye.

If I have time I'll redo all four hands . . . if not I can do a patch job on the one . . . or maybe just trim it down . . .

These irrelevancies ran through her mind as Shern's voice filled the room, an endless sound. For someone who tortured the language, he sure loved to talk.

"Many times I this message to you have delivered," he was saying. "Possible it not is a musician having for reasons that described have been."

Amarie snuck a glance at him through lowered lids. The owner of Shern's Palace was agit. ed, pacing back and forth as he talked and talked. He was such a disgusting-looking thing. Did it ever occur to him that maybe the reason no one came to his runey little bar was because they couldn't stand to look at this pale, waxy thing with an eye that never blinked? That maybe she was the only reason the place had any customers at all? That she was *saving* Shern from going under because she had talent and people came to hear her intricate four-handed music?

". . . night one more having," Shern was saying. Then he stopped and looked at her with a certain finality, as though expecting a response, and she had to admit she hadn't been listening.

"Sorry, Shern, go over that once more, will you?"

Shern's sallow complexion went to a peculiar yellow shade; she had learned this was the onset of anger. "To be listening necessary is," he spat. "Not do I talk for listening pleasure myself."

Amarie sighed. Part of her said, what the rune, get this miserable creature out of your life forever; but the other part ordered her to do anything—anything—to please Shern so he wouldn't cast her out without a job. *I can make him like me,* flashed desperately across her mind; *I can never like him* followed soon after.

Sometimes she thought honesty was one of her most troublesome traits.

"Shern," she said, "if you used the runey Universal Translator maybe I could figure out what you're trying to say, but since you don't, just butcher it one more time for me. All right?"

Shern's eye bored into her. "Clear making was, night one more having you are."

"Shern, maybe to you that's clear making, but to me it's confusing being. You telling me tonight's my last night?"

"Simple it is," said Shern, shrugging disdainfully.

"You mean to say that after all I've done for you, after I've built a clientele, a loyal following, people who come to the bar night after night just to hear me—you're going to get rid of me? The only attraction you have to offer?"

And then Shern smiled. At least that's what she thought it was—on Shern it looked like a grimace. But he was clearly quite self-satisfied when he announced, "Amazing talent finding am I. Dancer she is—with many legs having." Shern looked at her smugly.

Amarie stared at him. Was he kidding? This was his big idea for building business? A four-armed musician hadn't put Shern's place on the map of the sector, so he thought a multi-legged dancer was the answer? Amarie found herself laughing, a big, throaty, gutsy laugh—a bray, actually—that clearly caught Shern by surprise.

"Why laughing are?" he asked nervously. Shern hated being left out of things, and a joke he didn't get was always upsetting to him. That thought only made Amarie laugh harder.

"You runey little rune," she said when she had

finally caught her breath. "I am so runey glad to be getting out of your runey bar. I hope you and your runey dancer are miserable together."

And, still chuckling, she stood and walked out of his office. She knew Shern was staring after her, dumbfounded by her reaction—and that was a liberating thought. *I'll redo all my nails before tonight,* she thought, *and give myself a facial and maybe try that new metaphasic eye shadow. If this is my last night, it's going to be one rune of a performance.*

It was not until she got home to her tiny closet room that she burst into tears, and cried without stopping for an hour. Then she had to spend hours over a steam quill trying to reduce the swelling in her eyes; that took so much time she never did get around to repairing her fingernail.

Gretchen Naylor's green eyes flashed as she looked at Riker, and he had to fight feelings that he had somehow betrayed her. They were in the captain's ready room, where Riker had quickly led them after Naylor had come onto the bridge and requested a conference. That in itself was unusual; her attitude once they were secluded was nothing short of astonishing to him.

"I've been on this investigation from the beginning, Commander," she was saying now, "and I think I deserve to be included now."

"You've been extremely helpful. I know the contributions you've made, and I'm grateful. I'm just not sure it's wise for you to be seen at Shern's Palace."

"And that's because—?"

"You've been there once with me. You go again, you'll be noticed. *I'm* not going until Lieutenant Worf lets me know that an overweight Ferengi who likes 'Melor Famagal' has arrived."

"But when you go—if you go—I should be with you."

"I think I can handle the situation, Ensign."

The tone in Riker's voice got her attention. She fixed those eyes on him. "Am I overstepping the boundaries, Commander?"

"You're coming very close."

From the look on her face, he realized this statement frightened her—on some profound, visceral level. It was a brief flash of vulnerability, and then she became extremely composed.

"Sir, if I've seemed pushy, I apologize. I take my work seriously. It's important for me to do my best. I want the chance to prove myself, and it's hard for me to have those chances taken away."

Riker stared at her. He had a vision of a serious, dedicated little girl, studying obsessively at her desk while the warm, fragrant breezes of Indiana wafted through her room. Somewhere outside, in the lush gardens, her family worked and laughed together, bonding in their shared commitment to give this gifted child a chance to grasp a dream—Starfleet Academy.

The family had each other; they had a goal that held them together. Gretchen was alone, bearing the responsibility of fulfilling the vision for which her parents and her siblings gave so much. She had not only survived a journey that claimed many casualties —she had excelled. She was admitted to the Academy, graduated with honors, and then was posted to Starfleet's flagship. Gretchen Naylor was in rarefied company, the upper minuscule percentile of those millions in the quadrant who longed to be exactly where she was.

But did it bring her joy? And what had it cost her?

"Ensign Naylor, you've been invaluable in this investigation. I've valued your insights. I can honestly say we wouldn't be where we are if it hadn't been for you."

He had the sense that she drank these words as a dying man gulped water in the desert. Yet her expression remained impassive. "Thank you, sir. I hope my performance has been acceptable."

"More than acceptable. Exemplary."

She nodded briefly. A moment passed. "But my presence won't be required on Qualor?"

"I don't think it's wise."

"Very well."

She turned away and started to leave; he felt an overwhelming flood of protectiveness toward this driven woman, wanted to salve her feelings somehow. "Gretchen?"

She turned back to him. "Maybe we could have dinner some night. I'd like to know you better."

She stared at him, a proud tilt to her head. "Commander—please don't patronize me," she said. Then she walked out.

Amarie's puffy eyes had subsided by the time she went to work, and the metaphasic eye shadow, which changed color and design constantly, concealed any residual swelling. She had that awful snuffly feeling she always got when she had been crying for a long time, but all things considered, she thought she was looking pretty good.

The room, as usual, was nearly empty. The prostitutes (thank the rune she hadn't had to sink that far—yet) sat gossiping in the rear, enjoying the moments before the men began to drift in and demand companionship. Amarie walked through the field of unfilled tables and toward the spotlight that centered on her keyboard.

A new man was seated there.

She knew he was from the *Enterprise,* for he wore a similar uniform; he had been sent by Will Riker according to their plan. But she was unprepared for his powerful virility, and her heart thudded a bit as she looked at him. His bony ridge marked him as a Klingon; Amarie thought he was the most devastatingly attractive man she had ever seen.

She asked if there was anything special he wanted to hear.

"Do you know any Klingon opera?" he demanded.

Amarie thrilled to the assertiveness of his command. She wished she had studied more opera. Maybe she could improvise

"I don't get a lot of requests for it," she admitted, hoping this manly being would not think her unsophisticated for not knowing his music.

"Surely you must know at least one theme from *Aktuh and Maylota,*" said the Klingon.

Somewhere in the dim regions of her memory Amarie touched on one aria from the opera, a baritone's lament. It had been popular when her mother was young, and she had seen holographic recordings of it. Maybe she could retrieve enough of it to please this exciting man.

Her four hands trailed gracefully over the keys, finding the melody and gradually filling in accompaniment. "I may be a little rusty," she said, but surprisingly it was all coming back to her, and she began to play with increasing sureness. And then, unbidden, she began to sing, her throat opening to the achingly beautiful sentiments of the doomed love affair.

To her delight, a pleased expression appeared on the Klingon's face, and he nodded emphatically. Then he seemed to sink into a euphoric rapture, and from his throat a softly growling sound emerged as he began to hum. This aroused Amarie incredibly. Her mind began to hunt feverishly for other Klingon operas she might have heard.

"Maylota, Maaaay-lot-aaaaa," the Klingon bellowed. He had lost all sense of the place and had thrown back his head, pouring out the sorrows of an unrequited love in his rich *basso* voice. Amarie shivered. She wanted all time to stop, and to spend eternity in this moment, playing a love theme while her Klingon warrior sang at her side.

"What is that dreadful noise?" The harsh nasal voice knifed through the fetid air of the room like a laser. "It sounds like a Bardakian pronghorn moose."

The Klingon stopped singing and turned to see who it was who had interrupted his aria. Amarie knew only too well.

Omag the Ferengi was a regular at the bar, coming in every few nights. Why he came there she never understood, because Omag was so rich and powerful he could have bought the place and had it delivered to his dwelling.

He was also the fattest man she had ever encountered. He waddled toward a table, his rotund body stuffed, sausage-like, into an outfit so large it could have held four normal-size Ferengi. On either arm, as usual, were two striking women in skimpy, disgustingly revealing dresses. One had no back to it, the other almost no front, and the bottoms of the woman's breasts and all of her skinny stomach were open to the wind. Amarie sniffed slightly as she glanced at the two. They were cheap runey slatterns, as far as she was concerned, and far too thin. Those women could never bounce like Amarie.

Omag looked at her and gave her a nod. "You know what I want to hear," he announced, and took a seat. He couldn't draw his chair up close to the table because of his stomach, so he snapped his fingers and one of the women handed him a basket of palag crackers, which he immediately began stuffing into his mouth.

Amarie turned to the Klingon and gave him a slight nod, then began to drift into the familiar strains of Omag's favorite song, "Melor Famagal." She saw the officer casually touch the insignia he wore on his uniform, and softly say, "Worf to *Enterprise.*" No one except her could have heard him.

"Go ahead," came back a voice, and Amarie recognized Riker's quiet tones.

"A fat Ferengi has just entered the establishment," said the Klingon.

"Is that 'Melor Famagal' I hear?" asked Riker.

At Amarie's nod, the lieutenant answered, "It is."

"I'm on my way."

Amarie looked over to see Omag ordering food and drink—lots of it, if pattern held. Occasionally he glanced at her and smiled, nodding his ridiculous head, encouraging her to keep playing the runey song.

And Amarie did. She'd rather be playing love themes from operas and hearing the manly voice of the handsome officer near her, but Omag was always good for a big tip at the end of the evening. And if this was to be her last night of work, she'd need it.

The remembrance that by tomorrow she would be unemployed hit her with full force again. The thrill of meeting the Klingon had temporarily driven that depressing thought away, but it returned with grinding impact. What the rune was she going to do? She couldn't even get off this runey little planet. And there weren't any more jobs for four-armed keyboard players; she'd been lucky to find this one.

Amarie sighed and tried to concentrate on making sure Omag was happy with her playing. His tip might have to last her for quite a while.

Riker transported to the surface alone, trying not to feel qualms about leaving Gretchen behind on the *Enterprise.* Her summary rejection of his dinner invitation had stung, and he reflected that this was exactly the kind of unpleasantness he had wanted to avoid. He vowed from this point to keep their relationship on purely neutral ground.

But he had to admit that he had been deeply affected by the vulnerability he had seen exposed in her. Her need to achieve, to be the best, was a desperate and driving force, which, if derailed, left her defenseless.

It was a failing she would have to correct if she were going to make it in Starfleet. Needy people are susceptible people, and such people—particularly in security—make mistakes. Mistakes in Gretchen's branch of service could be life threatening, to herself and to others.

He shook off these dark musings as he entered the hideaway and heard the strains of "Melor Famagal" still playing. There were few patrons in the place, as usual; ahead he saw Worf seated near Amarie, who was managing to make the fourth time through the melody sound varied and fresh.

Riker's eyes roamed the room and easily found the fat Ferengi, Omag. He was seated at a table with two gorgeous women, stuffing food into his mouth at a prodigious rate, washing it down with what looked like champagne.

Worf caught Riker's eye and stood, walking casually toward him. The two men glanced toward Omag, who was now pounding the table with his shoe.

"Where is the waiter?" he was squealing, and bits of food fell out of his mouth as he did so. "Is there no waiter in this sorry place?"

Riker and Worf made their way to the table. Riker leaned down toward the fat little man and asked seriously, "Is there a problem?"

"Yes," snapped Omag. "I need more napkins." He turned away and slurped more champagne.

"Use your sleeve," said Riker quietly.

This produced the anticipated effect. Omag turned to him in shocked surprise, eyes wide. "What did you say?" he asked incredulously, as bits of food dangled from his mouth.

Riker found him disgusting. He glanced toward one of the lithe young women who were sipping drinks and pretending to ignore this little encounter. "Or use her sleeve, I don't care."

Omag's squinty eyes narrowed further. "Who are you?" he demanded.

"Commander William Riker, the U.S.S. *Enterprise.*"

"Am I supposed to stand up and salute?" Omag

looked at the women and laughed heartily. They joined suit.

"We're investigating the disappearance of a Vulcan ship—"

"You've got the wrong Ferengi. I never trade in Vulcan ships."

"We know you were involved," persisted Riker.

Omag stuffed something long and oily into his mouth and chewed for a moment before responding. "Who would want a Vulcan ship? Vulcans are pacifists. I deal in warships." A drizzle of oil squirted from his mouth and he wiped it with his hand. "Can somebody get me a napkin?!" he yelled.

Nobody did. "Who *would* want a Vulcan ship?" asked Riker, not letting him wriggle away.

"Hypothetically speaking?" Omag's eyes were wide in mock seriousness.

"Hypothetically speaking."

"I never learned to speak hypothetical." Omag tilted back his head and howled with laughter, spraying bits of matter over the table as he did. The women followed suit, laughing merrily.

Riker had had enough. He picked up the edge of the table and tilted it so that all the food and drink slid down and descended on top of the Ferengi and his women. They erupted in shrill shrieks of rage and dismay, leaping to their feet and brushing ineffectually at their sodden clothes.

Riker heard the music stop behind them. He moved toward the startled Ferengi, now looking ridiculous with food dumped all over him. "Are you crazy?" the man screeched. Riker grabbed him by his lapels and raised him off his feet. It was an effort to do so, but his adrenaline was pumping. He could sense Worf at his back, watching for any move from the patrons.

"Let me explain what's going to happen if you don't tell me about that Vulcan ship," he began, in a calm voice. "Your passage rights through this sector will be revoked. But more than that, I'll be very unhappy."

The Ferengi, his feet dangling inches over the ground, looked at him with a mixture of loathing and fear. "I delivered it to a Barolian freighter," he gasped.

"At what coordinates?"

"I don't remember."

Riker tightened his grip and the squat little man wheezed desperately. "Ow, watch it . . . you're stretching my neck . . ."

"Coordinates?"

"At Galorndon Core. Near the Neutral Zone. That's all I know. I swear it." His face was turning a strange purplish color.

Riker threw him back into his seat, directly on top of a creamy tart, which squished as the fat man landed on it.

"Enjoy your dinner," said Riker pleasantly. He turned to smile at Amarie, and as he and Worf started to leave, he picked up a napkin from a nearby table. He flung it toward Omag, and it landed on the wretched little man's lap. Riker was pleased to see that even Worf grinned at that.

Amarie stared at the scene of mayhem in dismay. The two Starfleet officers were gone, having left behind a powerful Ferengi ship dealer who was now sitting in the middle of his own dinner. The two concubines had disappeared, cleaning themselves up, she supposed. But what distressed her was the realization that this was not a night when Omag was going to leave a sizeable tip. He'd been roughed up, humiliated, and doused with food and drink—he probably couldn't wait to get out of there and he wasn't going to feel like throwing money around when he did.

As she looked over at him, she found herself feeling sorry for the runey little toad. He looked pathetic, daubing at himself with a napkin. The waiters had finally reappeared and were doing their best to clean up the food, and Shern hovered and clucked uselessly. The table and floor looked like a giant baby had just eaten dinner there, slopping food everywhere.

Without conscious thought, Amarie rose and went to Omag, took the napkin from his hand, and began wiping his head for him with one hand, his shirt with another; another patted his shoulder. "Too bad, Omag," she crooned. "Don't let it get you down." She tenderly wiped the folds of his huge ears.

"I'll hire guards. I'll go after them . . ." he was sputtering in his rage and distress.

"Pumply, they're long gone from here. They got business to do and they're already on their way. Besides, you don't want to waste your time on petty little runes like them. You could buy and sell them a thousand times over."

Omag frowned, reflecting on this. "It is true," he pronounced.

"You just settle down and forget about them. The evening is young and I haven't even got warmed up with 'Melor Famagal.' We'll get you set up at a new table and order some champagne. You ever try the fried Caldor eel? No? Oh, pumply, you haven't lived . . ."

She continued clucking over him, gently leading him to another table, all four hands brushing food from his clothes, seating him, and tucking a fresh napkin in his neck. "There," she cooed. "Pretend you just walked in the door and sat down and told me to play your song. Okay?"

Omag was undone by her tender ministrations. His eyes actually seemed moist as he stared up at her. "Amarie," he snuffled, "you are a good woman."

She laughed her horsey laugh; it felt good to laugh again. "You better believe it, Omag." She leaned down to him and whispered in one giant ear, "and I got more bounce to me than those skinny little girls you bring in here all the time."

Omag smiled and nodded, his eyes twinkling once more. "You play me 'Melor Famagal' about fifty or sixty times, I'll be myself again. And then"—he stretched up to her and she leaned down to hear—"we will have late dinner together. Just you and me. I think I would like to get to know you better."

Amarie gave him a squeeze and a smile, then made her way back to the keyboard. She felt a joyousness in her heart that she realized hadn't been there in a long, long time. She was eager to get her hands on the keys. That cute little rune was going to hear "Melor Famagal" like he had never heard it before.

Amarie knew that somehow, everything was going to work out just fine.

Chapter Seventeen

DEANNA TROI WAS AWARE of uncomfortable feelings between Will Riker and Ensign Gretchen Naylor. They were sitting in the conference lounge, being briefed by Will on the events at Qualor Two.

There was nothing overt that happened between Will and the pretty young ensign, but Troi's empathic senses were fully engaged by something potent and puzzling that she sensed, particularly from Gretchen. She noted that Will seemed to avoid looking at her, sweeping his eyes by her as he recounted the events of the previous night and the information he had garnered from Omag, a Ferengi ship dealer.

"He claimed to have delivered the ship to a Barolian freighter near Galorndon Core. And you know what that place brings to mind."

The rocky shoals of Galorndon Core had figured prominently in another adventure they'd had with the Romulans, a few years ago. Troi could remember well the tension that had been created on the *Enterprise* when they had found a downed Romulan craft on that bleak, storm-ridden planet and had faced down the Romulan captain, Tomalak, who claimed that the incursion into Federation space was accidental and insignificant.

They were sure that it wasn't, that the Romulans had their eyes on that prize location near the border of the Neutral Zone, but nothing was ever proven either way. And henceforth, the name of Galorndon Core had always conjured to them the image of Romulans.

"I think we should get this information to Captain Picard. It might somehow be related to his mission." This was Ensign Naylor speaking, carefully addressing the room and no one person in it.

"Agreed, Ensign," said Riker, also not looking at her. Troi found this strange, indeed. What was going on? Were these two having a romance—one that was going badly?

She found it hard to believe. She and Will had learned years ago that, if they were to serve on the *Enterprise* together, they had to sacrifice their own prior relationship. There was no place on a starship for such emotional entanglements. Surely Will had learned that lesson well enough not to repeat it. But there was definitely *something* going on between him and the beautiful ensign.

"Commander Data was going to work on a piggyback communication process in order to get transmissions out of the Neutral Zone," Riker was saying. "If he's successful, we can apprise them of our findings."

"Of course, we could go to Galorndon Core. See what's going on there." That from Ensign Naylor, again stated to no one in particular.

"Captain Picard expects us to be at Qualor. That piggyback transmission would never find us at Galorndon Core. We'll wait."

"Aye, sir," replied Naylor quietly, but Troi again felt a surge of—something—from the young woman. Not love, not romance . . . a *longing* for something was as close as Troi could get to it.

Troi's job on the ship was to help keep emotional harmony among the crew. It was a job with which she was feeling vaguely dissatisfied these days, but she took pride in doing it well and she wasn't about to let it slip. If she sensed something unusual going on with any of the crew, it was appropriate for her to figure out what it was and deal with it.

When Will dismissed the group, Troi made her way toward Naylor. "Ensign," she said in a friendly way, "I'd love to have tea with you sometime soon."

The younger woman looked taken aback for a brief moment, but then returned the smile. "I'd like that," she said, and what Troi picked up from her now, overwhelmingly, was relief.

"Why not now?"

". . . and there's never a time when I leave anything undone until the next day. If there's work on my desk, I do it before I go to my quarters."

Troi nodded and sipped at her tea. Gretchen Naylor was pouring herself out to Troi unabashedly; what Troi was hearing was a tale of a bright, motivated young woman who had set her sights on Starfleet and who never looked back in her single-minded drive to get there.

Only once she had, she couldn't turn herself off.

Ensign Naylor was inflicting a lot of self-made stress on herself in her need to be the best and the brightest.

Troi wondered if her family, when she was growing up, ever loved and praised her just because she was herself—or only because she was an exceptional student. Troi felt certain it was the latter.

Gretchen's feeling of self-worth was all bound up in her achievements. If she sensed that she was faltering at all, if she felt rejected, as she had felt by Will Riker when he wouldn't include her on an away team, it was an assault on her entire identity. That could be troublesome, for no one got through life without quite a few failures, rejections, and missteps. No one of them could be given such importance that it rocked the core of one's very being.

Troi sensed that this was basically a stable, intelligent woman whose focus was just a little obsessive. She needed something to draw her out of her preoccupation with success.

"Ensign, have you considered a hobby?" Troi was surprised when Gretchen burst out laughing, until the young woman explained that Commander Riker had suggested the very same thing. This made Troi smile.

"He was talking about playing something called a stand-up bass. Have you ever heard of it?" Troi smiled again. Will was always trying to get people to play musical instruments. He loved music so much he believed everyone else would get the same pleasure from it he did.

"Yes, I have. It's an ancient instrument."

"I just don't think that's anything that would hold my interest."

"Can you think of something that would?"

To Naylor's credit, she honestly struggled with the question. Troi had no doubt that she was searching within herself, trying to find an elusive something that might pull her out of her single-minded concern with achievement.

But eventually she shrugged. "Not really." She looked down at her hands for a moment and then asked, "What's wrong with my just wanting to do a really good job as a security officer?"

"There's nothing wrong with that," replied Troi. "But if that's *all* there is . . . then, ironically, you might not be as good a security officer as someone who has outside interests."

The young ensign nodded. She understood; she wasn't resistant. She simply didn't know of anything else that interested her except work.

"When you were a little girl," Troi suggested, "was there anything you enjoyed doing? Anything besides studying?"

Gretchen sat quietly, searching her mind, genuinely trying to recollect her childhood. "I was so lucky. My family gave me everything, sacrificed for me, let me have the time I needed to study. I owe them so much."

Troi studied Gretchen intently. Her heart went out to this resolute young woman, beset with overwhelming feelings of responsibility. Her whole family had given their lives to see her succeed—how could she let them down? She carried this burden with her every minute; she had to be the best, or it would invalidate all the sacrifice her family had endured.

"Your brother and sister . . . did you ever just—play with them? Children's games, that kind of thing?"

Ensign Naylor smiled. "Sometimes. Not a lot. There were always chores, and of course there was—"

She stopped and looked down, as though stricken.

"There was what?" Troi asked gently.

"Chores," repeated Gretchen, "all the time—we had acres of herbs, and of course there's a lot of work in natural herbs, weeding, weeds are awful since chemicals were outlawed, and everybody had to pitch in—"

"Gretchen," interrupted Troi, "what are you trying not to talk about?"

The green eyes stared at her. Troi saw deep-seated pain in that look; she knew she had tapped into something. Gretchen tried to laugh, but it came out in a strangled cackle. "What do you mean?"

"There was something else in your life, something you have trouble talking about . . ."

Ensign Naylor rose abruptly, paced the room, worked to control herself, and finally turned back to Troi. She seemed composed once more. "I guess you're talking about Casey."

Troi's head tilted. "Casey?"

"My brother. Baby brother. You probably read about him in my biographical profile."

"I haven't read your profile, Gretchen. I do that only if there's a problem."

"I see." Naylor looked as though she wished she hadn't brought it up.

"Tell me about Casey."

"He was sick. He died before he was two."

"Sick with what?"

The young woman hesitated. "I—don't know. My folks never talked about it much. It was hard on them."

"And how about you?"

"Pardon?"

"It must have been hard on you, too. How old were you when he died?"

193

A brief hesitation. "I was twelve."

"It must have been awful for you."

Gretchen Naylor seemed to be trembling slightly, mouth open, eyes focused on empty space in the room. She drew a breath, struggling once again for composure. "Actually, I didn't even go to the funeral. I had divisional tests that day."

And she burst into tears.

Troi offered her tissues and let her cry for a while, occasionally patting her shoulder and murmuring supportively. She knew the accumulated grief of years was coming to the surface, a mourning that had never taken place. Crying wouldn't erase that pain, but it would help bring it closer to the surface.

After a while, Naylor mopped at her face. Her words, when she spoke, were occasionally interrupted by bouts of fresh sobs. "I never got to take care of him. Everyone else held him, and took him for walks, and sang songs to him. I would hear them from my room while I was studying. But they wouldn't let me take the time from my work." She cried for a few minutes more, then looked up at Troi. "He was a beautiful little boy . . . so tiny and helpless . . . but he had eyes like mine. We were the only ones in the family with green eyes . . . and I always thought he belonged to me a little . . . but I hardly even got to hold him."

She rose and started pacing again. "Once I snuck into his room when everybody was asleep, and I sat by his bed all night and whispered to him, about how much I loved him and all the things we'd do together when he got well. The next morning I fell asleep in class, but I didn't care."

She stopped pacing and looked at Troi. "That night, he got a very high fever. Before they could bring it down, he went into convulsions, and . . . and he died. I loved him so much I thought my heart would crack into pieces. But I couldn't even go to his funeral."

She sat down again, wiping at her eyes. "I'm sorry, Counselor. I haven't thought about this in years."

"I'm sure that's true."

"This won't happen again, I promise you."

"I hope that's not so, Gretchen. You've never grieved for that little brother. It's time you went through that."

"I don't want to think about it."

"I know. But you must acknowledge the pain, not bury it."

Naylor took a great shuddering breath, tried a crooked smile. "We were talking about finding a *hobby,* and it turned into this."

And a thought struck Troi. "Do you think you might like to volunteer in the nursery?"

Naylor looked at her curiously. "The nursery?"

"There are always a number of babies being cared for there. Many of the couples on the *Enterprise* both work, and put their children in care centers during the day. The nursery is always looking for extra hands to hold and cuddle the babies."

Troi could feel Gretchen rolling the idea over in her mind, tasting it, trying it. "Maybe," she ventured.

Troi had an instinct that this young woman might take pleasure in giving care to a helpless creature. She had been cheated from so much of life, and certainly she had some healing to do regarding her baby brother. The nursery might be just the place for her.

Gretchen composed herself and, after promising to see Troi professionally for a few weeks, departed. Troi had an overwhelming sense of satisfaction. Being a counselor might not be the most exciting job on the ship, but when things happened right, there was nothing quite like it. This kind of fulfillment was buoying to her, and she imagined that even a captain like Jean-Luc Picard would value these small moments of triumph.

Riker was standing on the bridge of the *Enterprise*, looking at the viewscreen. There he saw the bridge of the Klingon ship *Kruge*, with Picard, Data, and the Klingon captain all in evidence. Riker had been running down his experiences at Qualor, and the information he had pried loose from the Ferengi dealer, Omag.

"As soon as I heard this Barolian ship was at Galorndon Core, I started to think Romulans," he concluded, and saw Picard absorb the intelligence and try to determine its significance.

"And the Romulans are suddenly very interested in bonding with the Vulcans," Picard mused. "Spock has been meeting with the new Senate proconsul about reunification."

Riker was stunned. A formal realigning of the Vulcans and Romulans? Such a possibility had never entered his mind. "Reunification?" he repeated lamely.

"The Romulan proconsul says he is prepared to endorse peace talks," Picard continued, and Riker found that statement even more surprising. A Romulan leader pushing for peace?

"What about Spock?" he asked.

"The ambassador is skeptical but he cares a great deal about reunification. As long as there's a chance of success, he will pursue it."

Troi spoke up. "I'm afraid I don't see where a stolen Vulcan ship fits into all this."

"Neither do I, Counselor." Picard's eyes sought out Riker again. "How soon can you be at Galorndon Core, Number One?"

Riker checked the calculations on his chair console. "Little over eight hours," he replied.

"It may be a wild-goose chase, but I don't think we have a choice, do you?"

"Agreed."

The image on the viewscreen suddenly began breaking up, and Riker saw Data turn from the console on the Klingon bridge. "We are losing our Romulan carrier wave, sir," he announced.

Picard turned to Riker once more. "We'll advise you further when you get there, Number One. Picard out."

The signal snapped out completely and Riker found himself looking at stars once more. He turned to the ensign at Conn. "Ensign, set a course to Galorndon Core. Take us to warp eight."

He settled into the command chair and watched as the stars turned from pinpoints to streaks as the massive ship jumped to high-warp speed. The solution to the mystery had been eluding him all along this journey. Maybe he would find the answer at Galorndon Core.

Chapter Eighteen

CAPTAIN K'VADA WAS ALL but salivating with glee. The android—that glorious creature who had returned his shoulder to its rightful position, where it was now mending nicely—had managed to tap into the Romulan information net. The possibilities this opened for K'Vada were infinite. He listened carefully as Picard and Data huddled over the computer where the android was accessing information.

"Captain, the Romulan subspace logs identify a transmission from the Romulan surface to a Barolian ship near Galorndon Core twelve hours ago."

Picard nodded as though this had some significance, and K'Vada felt compelled to set him right. "Galorndon Core is along the Barolian trade route. They trade a great deal with the Romulans. It's probably just routine."

But Data spoke up. "This would not appear to be routine," he asserted. "I have been able to trace the source of the transmission. It incorporates the code prefix of Romulan intelligence."

K'Vada's salivation increased. *Romulan intelli-*

gence! He would be lauded far and wide for bringing this plum to his people.

"Can you access it, Data?" Picard was asking.

Data's fingers flew over the controls. K'Vada noted that he functioned at a higher rate of speed than either humans or Klingons, and filed that away for future reference. "It appears to be a short sequence of numbers," he announced. "One, four, zero, zero."

Picard frowned. "Nothing else?"

"No, sir."

The Starfleet Captain paced for a moment, then turned back to them. "I want to advise the ambassador immediately. Mr. Data, you will accompany me to the surface."

K'Vada's temper flared a bit; now, just when he had everything at his fingertips, they were going to prolong this foolish mission! Picard was heading for the portal; he turned back and said to K'Vada, "Captain, maintain an emergency transport schedule at our beam-in coordinates."

K'Vada simmered. Not only would they not be able to leave here, but he had to act as a wet nurse to the two Starfleet officers, staying on alert until they decided to come back to the ship. The words were out of his mouth before he thought. "I do not take orders from you, Picard," he snapped.

He was unprepared for the response this produced. Picard turned on him and, in perfect Klingon, barked, *"P'tah J'ginQuol! Ktah!"* K'Vada blinked. The intensity of the oath was surprising.

"You will lock on those coordinates at sixty-minute intervals after our arrival."

K'Vada did not answer, and Picard and Data moved to the portal. K'Vada overheard the android say mildly, "That was not very Vulcan of you, sir." And they went out.

As soon as the portal had shut behind them, K'Vada began to laugh. He liked this Picard! Any human who could swear like that won his respect. And anyone who could stand up to K'Vada was a man who was not going to be stopped by the Romulans.

Picard and Data would be back on his ship. They would make their way through the Neutral Zone and then back to the Klingon home world. K'Vada would bring great honor to himself with his information about Romulan intelligence; he would spur the development of an artificial life-form and that would only enhance his position. He would give up the wandering life of a starship captain and settle down with K'kam —who would of course give up her own career to be with him—and they would live out their days in glory.

Captain K'Vada settled into his command chair. If only there were truly fresh *gagh* on this ship, everything would be perfect.

Spock was preoccupied when he entered Krocton segment, and so he didn't notice D'Tan until the boy was almost on top of him. "Mr. Spock!" D'Tan called. "I've been looking for you."

Spock almost smiled. This boy's fervid enthusiasm was infectious. "I have been meeting with the proconsul, D'Tan," he said. It was that meeting that had so occupied his thinking. He and Neral had spent several hours outlining the parameters of the discussions that would take place following their historic announcement that the worlds of Vulcan and Romulus would begin talks that might drastically alter the future.

"Does he still speak of reunification?" asked D'Tan, and Spock smiled at the unfettered idealism he saw reflected in D'Tan's eyes.

"He speaks of nothing else," he replied. *Nothing else,* his mind's voice repeated, though Spock was not certain why.

He and D'Tan moved to a table at the food court. The boy pulled some objects from his pocket—small, oddly shaped blocks with carving on each one. "Have you ever seen any of these?" asked the boy.

He lay them in Spock's palm, and the ambassador turned them over, inspecting them. "The syllabic nucleus of the Vulcan language," he said softly.

"They were my toys when I was small," explained D'Tan.

Spock stared at him. "Your parents wanted you to learn the Vulcan language?"

"As did their parents before them. To prepare for the day when we will live again with our Vulcan cousins."

Spock looked into the boy's eager face, and reflected in it he saw the possibilities of a glorious future—an era of peace among worlds, a reign of truth and contemplative tranquility. He was profoundly moved as he looked into the small, impetuous face.

He almost didn't notice when Jaron appeared in front of them and leaned in to speak quietly. "Your Federation friends have returned," he said. "They must see you immediately. I've told Pardek. He will meet you at the cave." Then Jaron moved off swiftly.

Spock rose and placed the small blocks in D'Tan's hand, then clasped the hand shut over them. He held the boy's hand for a moment, as though drawing strength from him, and then he turned and started for the caves.

Picard had waited anxiously until Jaron returned to tell him that he had been successful in contacting Spock; He was relieved when Jaron told him the ambassador would be there shortly. And Pardek was even now entering the caves, hurrying to Picard with a look of concern on his round face.

"What is it, Picard?" he asked worriedly.

"I'll wait until Spock gets here, Senator, if you don't mind. I'd rather brief you both at once."

"Of course."

"Intelligence gathered by my crew on the *Enterprise,* and by Commander Data. I hope it will prove to be nothing alarming."

"As do I, Captain." With that, Pardek retired to a side wall of the cavern and sat down heavily. Picard remembered that he was as old as Spock—well over a hundred years. Hurried, anxious visits to the underground caverns must take a toll on him.

Spock arrived minutes later, and Picard immediately launched into a recounting of the events that his first officer had encountered on Qualor Two—how a stolen Vulcan ship had been passed from hand to hand and was ultimately delivered to a Barolian freighter near a Romulan-controlled planet, Galorndon Core.

And then there was the message Data had uncovered, directly traceable to the Romulan intelligence unit, a message sent a few hours ago—to a Barolian freighter near Galorndon Core.

"The only communication that was sent," he said finally, "were the numbers one, four, zero, zero."

Pardek looked puzzled. "What does it mean?"

There was a brief silence, and then Spock's voice, sounding strangely weary, interjected. "It means," he said, "that the proconsul has apparently been attempting to deceive me."

Spock moved away from them, as though this betrayal were a physical anguish. "For what purpose I cannot say yet," he said. "But his conversations with me have obviously been part of a greater plan involving the stolen Vulcan ship."

"How do you know that, Ambassador?" asked Data.

"The time the proconsul has set for the subspace announcement of our peace initiative is fourteen hundred hours tomorrow. One, four, zero, zero."

Pardek looked puzzled. "But why would they need a Vulcan ship?" he queried.

"That will become clear very shortly." A woman's voice rang out through the caves, and all eyes turned toward the ramp leading to the entrance.

Picard's heart went cold when he saw her.

It was Sela.

Young and lithe, she strode down the ramp, her beauty radiant in the damp of the cave. Part Romulan, part human, her short, cropped blond hair glistened in the light of the kekogen lamps. She wore the uniform of a Romulan commander and held a disruptor in her hands. Her eyes were blue ice.

From all sides, Romulan guards entered, quickly taking Picard and Data's weapons and surrounding the small group of men. It was swift and well orchestrated. Picard realized with consternation that they had been set up for this capture.

He turned to face Sela. "Captain Picard," she

purred. Her voice was silken honey; it belied the evil of which she was capable. "Welcome to Romulus. I trust you've enjoyed your visit."

He did not respond. He would not play games with Sela. She smiled and glanced toward Data.

"And this is the android I have come to respect in battle." The irony in her voice may have escaped Data, who said politely, "Lieutenant Commander Data."

Sela. That he should encounter her again, here— was there some predestination involved? Some ordained fate that threw their lives into synchronous collision? And was she Tasha's daughter?

No matter. Whatever her genesis, she was a creature without conscience, and her presence in this underground chamber gave a frightening new twist to this situation.

Sela stared at the Starfleet captain known as Picard and felt an undeniable thrill of triumph. She had heard this man's name from the earliest time she could remember—and had grown up hating him. Her mother had talked of him constantly, as she did of all her fellow officers on the *Enterprise,* and Sela had gradually decided that each of those people was her blood enemy.

It was bad enough that her mother was human, and a common prisoner. That she failed to realize the honor that had been bestowed on her by General Meldet, who chose to mate with her—this was what Sela could not forgive. Her mother was not only foolish but unworthy.

Sela was the product of the union between the captured Starfleet officer and one of the highest-ranking generals in the Romulan guards. And during the brief part of her childhood while her mother still lived, she was subject to Tasha Yar's endless stories of the vast starship on which she had served, and the wonderful people she had worked with. It was a strange story, and Sela didn't fully understand it. Tasha kept saying that Captain Picard had sent her "from the future." Sela didn't know what that meant until she was older, and even then she couldn't comprehend it. But what Tasha had said was that her ship, the *Enterprise D,* had somehow encountered its counterpart from the past—the *Enterprise C.*

It was some kind of space-time distortion, obviously, and who could truly explain those? However it happened, her mother had been sent by Picard to join the *Enterprise C*—the ship from the past. And that ship was attacked by Romulan forces and destroyed, with all but a handful being killed immediately.

Tasha was one of those survivors. After standard interrogation, she had caught the eye of Meldet, who desired her. And, in order to spare her life and the lives of her fellow prisoners, Tasha Yar consented to become Meldet's consort.

Sela had been born a year later.

And, for over four years, heard the stories of the *Enterprise* crew.

Sela had probably loved her mother at one point; she couldn't remember it, but surely love had been there once. However, her adoration of her father was immediate and constant. He was powerful and exciting—tall, with a deep voice that Sela loved. Her father was feared and respected by everyone.

How could her mother not adore this man?

But she didn't. She tolerated him, but she did not

love him. And, one night when Sela was four, her mother had come to her in the middle of the night and, warning her to be very quiet, bundled her up and carried her out of their compound.

Only when they were outside did Sela realize that she was being stolen away, away from her beloved father, away from her home, away from everything she held dear.

And so she cried out for the guards.

Her father had offered this woman her life. He had given her a home, protection, a daughter. And how did Tasha Yar repay him?

With betrayal.

Sela stood with her father and watched as Tasha was executed. Everything in her that was human died with her mother that day. All that was left was a Romulan, who burned with the desire to destroy the crew of the *Enterprise,* those to whom Tasha had been loyal. Those who had caused her to betray Sela's father.

And now, standing in this damp cave, looking at the astonished faces before her, Sela realized that she had the glorious Picard in her power. She would see if he measured up to all her mother's overblown praise. She doubted it. Before she was through, he would be revealed for the petty, inadequate human that he was.

And Sela's lifelong dream would be realized.

As Picard stood in the harsh white glare of the kekogen lamps, staring into Sela's cold, gleaming eyes, Picard realized that his and Spock's instincts about Neral had been correct. The proconsul had been leading them on, baiting them and drawing them in so that he could, ultimately, apprehend them. The vaunted peace talks were never intended to take place; reunification was nothing more than an idealist's dream.

Picard looked at Spock. The ambassador's face looked gray and worn, as though he bore the full brunt of this calamity. Exhaustion showed in every line of his craggy face; defeat seemed to be crushing him.

"How could they know of this location?" Pardek was beseeching Spock. "Someone betrayed us."

"Yes." Spock's voice was flat. "You did."

Picard's look snapped toward Spock. The ambassador was boring into Pardek, and the senator was trembling. "Spock," he said, aghast, "we've been friends for eighty years."

But, unmoved and stolid, Spock gazed back at him. "It is the only logical conclusion. You invited me to Romulus. You arranged the meeting with the proconsul. And you knew that Picard and Data had returned to the surface with new information."

Pardek shook his head, trying to maintain the innocent front, but Sela's throaty laugh obviated the effort. "The great Spock," she said, not without admiration. "Very well. Senator Pardek, your service to the Romulan people is noted and appreciated."

Pardek seemed to deflate a little. He looked right into Spock's eyes.

These men have been friends for eighty years, thought Picard. *Has Pardek been using Spock all that time, lying in wait, hoping for the opportunity to take advantage of that friendship? Was that all it ever was?*

Spock and Pardek were holding a look. It must have connoted nearly a century's relationship. It culminated when Pardek said ruefully, *"Jolan tru,* Spock."

There was no sense of discomfort, or of acknowledgment of the long friendship. Pardek had simply severed the bonds. Nothing more.

"Do not be distressed," Sela said to Spock. The ambassador was not looking at her, Picard observed, and she spoke to his ear. "Your dream of reunification is not dead. It will only take a slightly different form—the Romulan conquest of Vulcan."

She nodded to the guards, and they prodded the trio up the ramp.

D'Tan would never be able to say what it was that cautioned him to take refuge in the ground-level storage unit he had discovered years ago. It was nothing tangible, just a sense of unusual anticipation in the hot, heavy air; a kind of compression as though distant explosions were felt, rather than heard.

Others had premonitions, too, he was sure. There was a restiveness on the street, little eddies of scurrying activity that sprang up and dissipated in random patterns. A Circassian cat that belonged to a shopkeeper prowled her window restlessly, arching her back and spitting.

D'Tan's hiding place had a grate that opened on to the street and provided a view. When he was a very small boy he had discovered that he could wriggle into this space between the storage unit and the facade of the building and lie undetected for hours, watching the panorama of the streets unfold before him. Now that he was older, it was becoming a tighter fit; and he had realized sadly that in another year or two he would have to give up his childhood retreat.

He had had an aimless day, first wandering the

neighborhood for several hours, looking for Mr. Spock, hoping to show him the language blocks. After Spock left to go to the caves, D'Tan spent some time with his friend Janicka, helping her clean her family's store. They had given him a meal and a piece of fruit to take with him.

It was that indefinable heaviness in the air that finally sent him crawling into the hiding place. He was uneasy; his stomach felt sick and he wondered if the fruit he had eaten was spoiled.

Sitting cross-legged in his hiding place calmed him down; it always did. He loved watching the passersby on the street, the little dramas that played out before him. There was a heady feeling of omnipotence that he could see without being seen, though D'Tan knew that if his parents discovered this little activity, they would probably not approve.

D'Tan saw Janicka walk from her parents' shop toward the food court. Janicka loved sweets, and her parents kept her on a strict limit. D'Tan knew they must be occupied now, and Janicka was sneaking away to get some forbidden treat. He watched as she spoke to the food keeper, who returned a moment later with *sesketh,* a sugary confection twisted on a spice stick. D'Tan almost laughed out loud, because he knew of all the treats Janicka's parents least liked her to have, *sesketh* was at the top of the list.

Now she'd have to finish it before she returned to the shop; she sat on an embankment as she nibbled daintily at the sweet. D'Tan observed that Janicka was one of the few people he knew who could eat and still look delicate. He'd never had such a thought before, and as his mind considered her gentle face and her large, dark eyes, he found himself thinking of Janicka in an entirely new manner.

It was while he was absorbed in this unaccustomed exploration of Janicka's attributes that he heard the first scream.

It was a woman, and she was not within his sight. But he saw others on the street react to the scream and look off, to his right, down the thoroughfare that led out of Krocton segment.

Within seconds there was more noise—unfamiliar, disturbing—a clamor of shouting and more screams.

D'Tan's stomach twisted with fear. Whatever was happening, he knew it was worse than anything he had ever experienced. Now the people on the street before him were running, becoming crazed, colliding with each other in desperate haste. Some ran to his left, simply trying to get away from whatever was approaching; others ran the opposite way to look for loved ones or to take sanctuary.

The clamor of noise to his right was increasing in volume, and soon he could hear a pounding of footsteps—hundreds of them, many the harsh stamping of military boots as they marched inexorably down the street.

Then he caught the unmistakable sound of disruptor fire. He shrank back in his hiding place in fear. Disruptors were one of the most terrible weapons ever invented; were they being used on innocent citizens?

The next thing he saw was a flood of terrified people, running, stumbling, some glancing back over their shoulders as they ran, all wild-eyed, all fleeing some awful and as yet unseen monstrosity.

One woman stumbled and fell; the crowd marched

over her, ignoring her pleas for help and then her frantic screams as she was trampled. Finally she was still; D'Tan could see only her outstretched arm, fingers twitching faintly.

Then came the guards.

Neral's security guards were the most feared unit of the military. They were chosen first on the basis of size and strength; once tapped for service, they underwent special adaptations of their brain chemistry that reduced any sense of conscience or empathy. Then their plan centers were regulated so that their bodies were impervious to the torment of physical injury.

The result was a brutal creature without compassion, who would follow orders relentlessly, would not be slowed by injury, and would fight tenaciously until the body itself simply gave out.

These were the beings that marched through Krocton segment now.

Faces impassive, dressed in iron gray uniforms, they moved like a relentless swarm of insects over a field, destroying it utterly. Disruptor fire lacerated buildings and caused them to tremble violently; some collapsed in on themselves. Glass shattered and exploded, often showering the frightened citizens with lethal shards.

Some guards amused themselves by nipping at the fleeing civilians with disruptors; a full setting would vaporize anyone, so obviously they had purposely set their weapons at a low level. Those who were unlucky enough to get grazed by the ugly blast dropped in their tracks, screaming in agony as their internal organs began to explode.

All this D'Tan watched with horror, not wanting to

see but unable to look away. It was a living nightmare of cruelty and mayhem, unfolding in bitter, bloody detail directly in front of him.

A gap in the guards' ranks opened briefly, and he saw Janicka, standing opposite him on the embankment, staring, frozen, at the havoc before her. "Run, Janicka!" he shouted, oblivious for the moment to his own safety. But his cry had no chance of being heard by either the guards or by Janicka; the devastation of the streets overwhelmed any other sound, and D'Tan's cry blended with the piteous wails of too many others.

And so he watched, riveted, as a guard noticed Janicka and ran toward her. The little girl stared up at him, unable to move. He picked her up and slung her over his shoulder, and then Janicka came to life. She shrieked, and kicked at the guard with all her might. Annoyed, he simply grabbed her by her ankles and swung her around in a circle until her face collided with the corner of a building.

He dropped her then and she crumpled, leaden, onto the street. Even from his hiding place, D'Tan could see that Janicka's fair, delicate face was now a template of cracked and broken segments through which blood was streaming. She did not move or even twitch. She would never again eat a treat or walk with him to the caves or clean the windows in her parents' store. Janicka, his good friend, was gone.

D'Tan sank back against the wall of the storage unit. The guards had already passed by, continuing their carnage as they marched through the segment. Here, before D'Tan, was a wasteland of the dead and wounded. Already the noise was subsiding, and all he could hear were the groans of those who still breathed.

He knew that Mr. Spock was in terrible danger. This massacre was meant to wipe out the movement, and if the guards knew that Krocton segment contained its nucleus and its most dedicated adherents, there was every chance they knew about the caves, too.

D'Tan waited a few moments until the noise of the marauding guards had grown faint, and then he crawled out of his sanctuary. Trying not to look at the devastation around him, he started running toward the caves.

Chapter Nineteen

THE *ENTERPRISE* CAME gracefully out of warp speed and
entered orbit around Galorndon Core. It was a bleak,
forbidding planet, electromagnetically shrouded and
obscured by fierce storms and wildly erratic arcs of
jagged electricity.

Riker turned from the viewscreen to Geordi, at one
of the aft science stations. "Any signs of life, Mr. La
Forge?" he asked.

Geordi shook his head as he scanned the instruments. "Negative, Commander."

"The Romulans could have a cloaked base on the
surface," suggested Troi.

"Or anywhere else along the Neutral Zone," added
Riker. He had an unsettling feeling of disappointment. He had felt they were close to uncovering the
mysterious origins of the stolen Vulcan ship, and now
they found themselves in orbit over an uninhabited
planet. Had they come all this way for nothing?

"Sir," Worf's voice interrupted, "a coded subspace
signal from Romulus. It's the captain."

Riker moved to Worf's tactical console, read the message to himself. Troi must have seen the concern on his face, because she moved toward him.

"What?" she asked.

Riker read the message aloud. "Maintain position at Galorndon Core. Diplomatic initiative appears to be succeeding. Will advise soon."

Riker found this message instantly suspicious. The captain had only been able to communicate with them from the Klingon ship, and then by piggyback transmission. This coded message directly from Romulus was troubling. He cast a glance toward Worf; he could tell that the Klingon officer shared his concern.

"The message did employ the proper code sequence, Commander," Worf said.

"Yeah," said Riker. "I'm sure it did."

But he still didn't trust it.

D'Tan was prepared for anything as he approached the caves. He kept cover as he neared them, running in a crouch through a thicket of dense *wagi* brush that paralleled the road. He stopped opposite the cave opening and watched for a while; he was apprehensive about entering and being caught in the narrow, tubelike chamber that led into the main cavern.

After a few moments, he decided not to risk the larger entrance but to take the time to come in from the rear, through a circuitous, winding corridor, which only he and a few others knew about, and which only children could navigate successfully because the openings in many cases were small.

In a few minutes he had reached the rocky ledges that traversed the hills rising above the subterranean caves. He lowered himself into a hole concealed by thorny bushes, then scurried down the shaft, and dropped into a small chamber. Three circular openings were grouped on a far wall; D'Tan took the middle one and wriggled through a long, narrow passageway. That was the hardest part, and once he had emerged he was only minutes away from the main chamber.

As he neared it, he walked carefully, listening for any sounds of disturbance; he heard nothing. Gingerly, he made his way down the corridor toward the cavern, one step at a time, listening between each step . . . then he stepped around the corner and into the cavern.

Someone attacked him with a rock.

Instinctively he threw up his arms and the blow glanced off his forehead, but still with enough force to drop him to his knees. The wound spouted blood and D'Tan scrambled backward, holding up his hands to defend himself.

It was Shalote, a friend in the movement. Her eyes were wild and she held another rock in her hand, ready to attack again. She stared at him. "D'Tan?" she asked incredulously, and lowered her hand.

"Shalote, there's been a massacre in Krocton segment. The guards killed everybody. . . . It was awful . . ." Now that he saw a friend, the terrible events came pouring out. He longed to be comforted, held, and soothed until some of the dreadful images left his mind.

But Shalote was staring at him, nodding, herself as traumatized as he. "It was the same here," she whispered. "The guards came and took everyone. I had been carrying water to the main cavern and I heard the commotion and hid."

"Mr. Spock . . . Captain Picard?"

"They were captured. I saw them being led out."

D'Tan sank to the ground. He wanted very much not to cry in front of Shalote, who was older and whom he admired, but he was in despair. He had no idea if his parents had survived the slaughter in Krocton segment, if his friends were alive or dead. Janicka was gone . . . how many more of his beloved companions had perished that day?

But the worst thing of all was the death of the dream. What he had hoped and longed for all his life, what he thought he would see happening in his lifetime—that vision was shattered. His people would continue to live the bleak and violent lives of Romulans, shut off from the rest of the quadrant, never coming to know their gentle Vulcan cousins.

D'Tan realized he had already started crying, sitting on the floor of the cave, tears flooding in an endless current. Shalote was crying, too, and eventually they held each other and sobbed for a long time, drawing what comfort they could from each other's presence.

An almost tangible sense of well-being suffused Commander Sela on this warm Romulan afternoon. Everything was going as it should. Spock, Picard, and the android Data had been taken at the caves, and that alone would have been enough to make her feel satisfied.

But she had also learned that the extermination process in Krocton segment had been successful. The area had been decimated, with hundreds dead and scores wounded. Never again would Krocton segment be a pocket of sedition.

Now, as she worked at her padd, she prepared to lay

the final chip in the plan on which she had spent the past five years. It was all within her grasp. The most difficult elements were already in place; what remained was relatively easy. And then the heady rewards of conquest would be hers.

She heard the door open and knew that Spock, Picard, and Data were being led in. She purposely didn't look up; it amused her to keep writing, all but ignoring them. Idly she said, "Come in, gentlemen. Take a seat, please."

As she concentrated on the padd, she was aware that the guards ushered the prisoners to chairs opposite her desk; they sat. Now she looked up at the guards and nodded to excuse them.

Sela smiled as she scrutinized the three men who sat before her. Spock and Picard were solemn-faced, refusing to reveal whatever emotions they might be feeling. The android, of course, had no emotions, and was sitting placidly, watching her. She went back to her writing as she said, "Excuse me. I'm just finishing up a speech. For you, Mr. Spock."

Presently, she put the padd down and leaned back in her chair. "I rather enjoy writing. I don't get to do it often in this job."

"Perhaps you would be happier in another job," offered Data, and she had to suppress a smile. She was intrigued by this unusual creature, and could even understand the fondness her mother had expressed for him. Sela herself had encountered him in different circumstances, and blamed him—and Picard—for her failure to sway the Klingon civil war in favor of her cohorts, Lursa and B'Etor. It was delightful to have both these Starfleet men in her custody; there would be time for proper, and prolonged, retribution.

Picking up the padd, she circled the desk and handed the implement to Spock. "Please feel free to change any words that you wish. I've tried to make it sound Vulcan . . . a lot of unnecessarily long words."

No one smiled. Spock began to read the padd. "In a few hours," she continued, "you will deliver this statement alongside our senate proconsul, Neral. It will announce to the Vulcan people that a peace envoy is on its way from Romulus. We will transmit it on all Federation subspace frequencies."

Picard spoke first. "A 'peace' envoy in a stolen Vulcan ship . . ." he breathed, and Sela could tell he had fit in a piece of the puzzle. She was only too happy to provide the rest. It was a wonderfully clever scheme, and she was proud of it.

"Actually, three Vulcan ships, Captain. The *Enterprise* is aware only of the one we stole from Qualor Two." She smiled at his look of surprise. "Yes, we've been following their investigation. It has forced us to make some minor changes, including a message that was sent in your name, ordering them to stay where they are."

Picard's astute eyes swept her face. "The moment those Vulcan ships appear in the Neutral Zone, the *Enterprise* will move to intercept." Sela almost laughed. She *loved* this—it was worth the five arduous years of planning. She had them at every turn.

"In that event," she purred, "the *Enterprise* will be given more important matters to attend to." She waited so she could enjoy the puzzled frustration on Picard's face. He was learning that Sela had thought of every eventuality and had provided for it. He would never underestimate her again.

She circled now toward the windows of her office,

and gazed out across the lofty spires of the city of Dartha. She knew that far below, the people lived in dark squalor, but here, above the streets, her view was of a maze of soaring towers, stately and pristine.

"In the meantime," she continued, turning back to the trio, "Ambassador Spock will be telling his people to welcome the peace envoy, and when they do, our forces will seize control of the Vulcan government before anyone realizes what has happened."

"Can you possibly believe that the Federation will not immediately intervene?" The question from Picard was more a flat declaration.

"Of course it will," responded Sela, relishing these moments, savoring the feeling of thwarting the great Jean-Luc Picard. "And we're fully prepared for that. But we'll *be* there. Entrenched. And it will be very difficult to get us out once we are. A new Vulcan government will be formed that will embrace their Romulan cousins." She paused, and then said, with a trace of irony, "Reunification will become a fact of life."

Spock had finished his perusal of the document she had written, and as he handed it back to her, he said dryly, "I will not read this or any other statement."

"If you do not, you will die. All of you will die."

"It is logical to conclude that you will kill us in any event. Therefore, I choose not to cooperate."

Sela was annoyed. "I hate Vulcans," she snapped. "I hate the logic. I hate the arrogance."

But of course she had considered this eventuality and provided for it as well. She walked toward a computer console. "Computer," she said, "holographic program Spock One." And then she turned to see how her three prisoners would react, and her feeling of well-being returned.

Picard turned as he heard the characteristic hiss that signaled the appearance of a holographic figure. He knew what Sela had done and was sure the others had anticipated it, too.

Standing in the room was a perfect representation of Spock. He was immobile now, frozen in a moment of serene meditation, his eyes focused on nothing. "By taking advantage of holographic sampling these last few days," explained Sela, "we have created a programmable Spock." She searched the faces of the men, seeming to want a reaction. Picard carefully kept his face expressionless; he had no desire to stroke this shrewd woman's ego.

"Run program," she said, and the holo-Spock came to life.

"This is Ambassador Spock of Vulcan," it announced, its voice a perfect representation. "By now, Federation sensors are tracking three Vulcan ships crossing the Neutral Zone. These ships carry the future of the Vulcan and Romulan people. Our long conflict is finally over . . ."

"Freeze," said Sela, and the figure stopped in midsentence. She adopted a vaguely disappointed look when she said, "We would have preferred an interactive Spock who could have responded to questions, but this will have to suffice." She smiled contentedly. She reminded Picard of an animal who has feasted after a kill, belly full and needs assuaged, at one with its world, sanguine and assured.

Picard felt impelled to rattle this self-satisfied attitude. "This will hardly convince anyone," he said tersely.

"I don't need to convince them," she explained. "Just confuse them long enough for us to reach Vulcan." She turned and gazed fondly at her creation, then said, "End program." The holo-Spock disappeared.

She smiled again—that annoying, lazy smile—and started for the door. "If you will excuse me," she said pleasantly, "it is time to send the ships on their journey." And she exited.

Immediately the three began to examine the room for escape potential. It didn't seem to offer any; it was an inner office and well sealed. "Suggestions?" asked Picard, almost automatically.

"Commander Data," mused Spock, "are they still unaware that we have access to their computers?"

"I believe so, sir," replied Data.

"Then perhaps you and I can find a way to create a diversion." Spock and Data moved toward the computer console, and for the first time in many hours, Picard began to hold a measure of hope.

The crew on the bridge of the *Enterprise* had been sitting in tense silence for an hour. Since arriving at Galorndon Core, they had each taken a few hours off to nap, but otherwise they had kept their posts.

They weren't even sure what they were waiting for. Riker felt like a coiled spring, his neck beginning to ache from the pressures of internal stress. "Maintain position," the captain's message—if that's what it was—had said. But why? "Will advise soon," it had continued, but that had been ten hours ago. How long were they to wait? And for what?

Riker had managed to take an hour and have coffee with Gretchen Naylor, briefing her on the latest developments and offering to let her wait on the bridge with them. To his surprise, she declined the offer, assuring him that she knew the situation was in good hands. There was a relaxed quality to her that he hadn't noticed before, and it flattered her. They arranged to have dinner once this present crisis had resolved itself.

Now, sitting in silence on the bridge, listening to the faint electronic hum and crackle that was the normal background noise of the instruments, his nerves were taut. More than anything, Riker hated to wait.

Worf's voice, when he spoke, startled them all. "Commander, sensors are picking up three vessels crossing the Neutral Zone." He paused, and then added, "Vulcan ships."

Troi whirled on him. "Vulcan?" she said, astonished. Riker was already on his way to the aft science station, where Geordi stood.

"What's their heading, Mister Worf?" Riker asked even before he reached Geordi.

"One-four-three, mark zero-one-two," replied Worf, and by the time Riker reached the science station, a grid on the monitor displayed the boundaries of the Neutral Zone, and Riker observed three small blips moving through it.

"That would put them on a course to Vulcan," said Geordi. He stared at the blips for a moment, keying commands on the console.

"Worf, signal them on subspace. Request their status. Geordi, see if you can tell if one of them is the ship we've been looking for." Riker saw Geordi and

Worf both spring into action. He realized his neck was feeling better already.

Worf reported first. "They say they're escorting a peace envoy from Romulus to Vulcan, sir. They request that we monitor Federation subspace channels. Ambassador Spock will be making an announcement shortly."

"Perhaps his reunification talks were successful," suggested Troi.

But it didn't feel right to Riker. A stolen Vulcan ship delivered near Galorndon Core . . . now Vulcan ships crossing the Neutral Zone *from* Romulus . . .

He turned to La Forge. "Geordi?"

"None of the transponder signatures match up to the missing ship, Commander. They might have been altered. I'll keep checking."

Riker pondered for a moment, then decided there was nothing to be lost by putting himself in position in case there was something rotten in Romulus.

"Set a course to intercept the Vulcan ships," he said, and saw Worf's head spin around.

"Sir," protested the Klingon, "the captain's orders were to maintain—"

"I know the captain's orders, Lieutenant. Engage."

The great ship whipped into warp speed, and Riker began to feel better. At least he was *doing* something.

When Sela had dispatched the ships across the Neutral Zone, she had purposely delayed returning to the office where Spock, Picard, and Data waited. She liked the idea of toying with them, giving them time to ponder their failure and her triumph, and to dwell uncomfortably on just what fate she planned for them. She knew they must be well aware of Romulan rituals of execution, and some time to consider their tolerance for those elegant customs might leave them in a less arrogant mood.

She was still undecided how to treat the android. He could feel neither pain nor emotion, so he did not fit comfortably into the rigorous plans she had for the other two. She wondered if he would be adaptable to Romulan use; he might make a worthwhile aide if his circuits could be reintegrated so that he lost his attachment to Starfleet and its doctrines. She would have to check with their robotic scientists about that. If so, she would keep Spock and Picard alive long enough to witness the subversion of their colleague.

So it was with a light heart that she entered her office to confront her prisoners once more.

And discovered that the room was empty.

Stunned, she and the guards quickly drew their disruptors and inspected the room. The prisoners were nowhere to be found. "Impossible," she breathed. "There's no way they could have gotten out of this room."

And then, more incredibly, a voice behind her barked, "That's far enough." She whirled to see Riker, Picard's first officer, with several of his security forces, all with phasers trained on them. "Hold it right there," snapped Riker. "Drop your weapons."

Instinctively, Sela acted, moving casually toward her desk, looking for cover.

"Drop your weapons," repeated Riker.

But she dropped to her knees and, using her desk as cover, she fired a burst toward them; her guards immediately followed suit.

But Riker and his men still stood. "Drop your weapons," repeated Riker, and suddenly Sela understood. She rose, waved toward her men. "Cease fire," she ordered, and walked closer toward Riker. "Holograms," she said with irritation, angry that they had been deceived.

What happened next happened so quickly that Sela felt as if she were watching a high-speed video log. A *hand* emerged from the wall—how can that be? her mind wondered—and clasped one of her guards at the neck; he crumpled onto the floor. The rest of Spock then followed the hand through the wall and took the guard's disruptor.

At almost the same time, Picard burst through the wall, too, and took another guard down with a short, vicious punch.

By this time Sela had recovered from her shock and raised her disruptor to aim it at Picard—but suddenly there was Spock, right on top of her, holding the disruptor he had confiscated from her guard.

"I'm afraid," he said with mock apology, "that I don't know too much about Romulan disruptor settings."

They eyed each other for a long moment as Sela considered the options. But no matter what way she came at it, she realized Spock could fire on her. She would either vaporize, if the setting were high, or die an agonizing death as her organs exploded if the setting were low.

She dropped the disruptor.

Spock glanced at Picard and said something very strange; it sounded like "Cowboy diplomacy." Whatever it was, it meant something to the two, because Picard acknowledged the statement with a slight smile.

Then Picard called out, "Well done, Mr. Data—

although I'm afraid you didn't get Commander Riker's hair quite right."

And suddenly the wall of her office disappeared—revealing the true wall, and the android at her computer console, having created a hologram of the wall behind which they had been hiding all along.

"I will be more observant in the future, sir," said Data.

How pleased with themselves they all were! How clever they believed themselves. Well, let them congratulate each other all they wanted; Sela's plan was still running smoothly.

"It doesn't matter what you do now," she informed them. "Spock's announcement will be made in minutes. Our forces will be on Vulcan before you can alert anyone."

And she was delighted to see the looks of consternation on their faces.

By Riker's calculation, they were within twenty minutes of intercepting the Vulcan trio of ships when they received the message from Dulisian Four. He had immediately contacted Doctor Beverly Crusher and she had come to the bridge.

"Commander?" she queried.

"Doctor, we've just received a priority-one distress call from the colony on Dulisian Four—a massive failure of the environmental support system. They're going to require evacuation and they already have injuries."

Riker knew that the Dulisian colony was comprised of over four hundred people. Without their environmental support system, the sealed colony could not sustain life. The *Enterprise* was within range of the

Dulisian system and could easily evacuate and transport the colonists.

But that would mean changing course and letting the Vulcan ships proceed on their way without challenge.

What to do? He had no right to interfere with the Vulcan convoy, but he was mighty suspicious of it. A friendly hail, a query about intentions—these were accepted protocol in space.

On the other hand, all he had regarding those ships was a hunch. An instinct. A gut feeling. And what was happening on Dulisian Four was real.

"Worf, are there other ships in the vicinity of the Dulisian system?"

The tactical lieutenant checked his readings, then announced, "One, sir. A Rutian archaeological vessel."

That would be a surveyor ship, much smaller and less well equipped than the *Enterprise.* Beverly echoed his thoughts, saying, "I'm sure it's not equipped to handle something of this scale, Will." And of course it couldn't.

Riker moved back to the aft station, where Geordi was monitoring the progress of the Vulcan ships. "La Forge, anything more on those ships?"

"I've checked every sensor display backward and forward," he replied. "If the Romulans altered them, they didn't leave any fingerprints. I can't tie any of them to the surplus yard."

"The Vulcan ships have entered Federation space, sir," announced Worf. "Maintaining course and speed."

There was no choice. He had absolutely no hard evidence linking the Vulcan ships to the one he'd been trailing. He had no reason to believe that trio of ships was anything other than what it said it was—a peace envoy proceeding to Vulcan to open talks of reunification. And on Dulisian, people were going to start dying.

"Lay in a new course," he commanded, "for Dulisian Four."

The ensign at Conn complied, but before Riker could give the order to proceed, Worf's voice broke in. The Klingon's voice held a note of urgency. "Incoming message from Romulus—on all subspace channels."

"On screen," Riker ordered.

And on the viewscreen there appeared the august presence of Ambassador Spock. The bridge grew quiet as everyone listened intently to his message.

"This is Ambassador Spock of Vulcan," he began. "By now, Federation sensors are tracking three Vulcan ships crossing the Neutral Zone."

The calm way in which he announced these measured words made Riker assume that he was going to announce the peace initiative. So it was with astonishment that he heard the Vulcan say, in his next sentence, "These ships carry a Romulan invasion force and must be stopped. I repeat, these ships—"

The image was suddenly scrambled and then it disappeared altogether. Riker was on his feet.

"Doctor, contact Dulisian Four and confirm that distress call. I have a feeling it may prove to be a false alarm." He saw from the corner of his eye that Beverly had already started for the turbolift.

"How long will it take to intercept those Vulcan ships, Mr. Worf?" asked Riker, returning to his command chair.

"Fourteen minutes, sir," Worf responded.

So that was it. It was all coming down to a confrontation fourteen minutes from now—the whole circuitous route they had followed, from Vulcan to Qualor Two to Galorndorn Core; the encounters with Klim Dokachin, with Amarie and Omag—it was all leading to this final challenge. Riker's heart was beating harder; his mind was racing, preparing options. He drummed his fingers on his leg, unconsciously.

He couldn't wait.

Chapter Twenty

SPOCK KNEW that his announcement had been terminated abruptly; he just hoped enough had gotten out to alert the people of Vulcan. He glanced at Data, who was still at the computer, working to ascertain if the transmission was successful. Picard still held the disruptor on Commander Sela.

Data turned to them. "Communication lines have been terminated at the transmitter," he declared. "But I am quite certain the message was sent prior to the interruption."

"Well done, Mr. Data," said Picard, still keeping an eye on Sela. Spock noted that he seemed to take some pleasure in having bested this clever young woman; they seemed to have some prior history, and he thought he would have to ask Picard about that someday.

"You'll never get out of this building," insisted Sela, two bright spots of color on her cheeks. She was maintaining a contemptuous attitude in spite of the apparent disruption of her plans.

"I disagree, Commander," Data told her civilly. "After studying the design of this structure, I have determined that our best route of escape would be the underground exit to the east of this wing. I have disconnected certain security scanners to assist us."

Spock saw the color in her face darken again, and her eyes sweep toward the console that contained the security circuitry.

Data moved from the console and looked at Sela almost apologetically, and said, "I am afraid we cannot permit you to warn your guards."

And then he did something extraordinary. He performed the Vulcan pinch on her. Spock watched as Commander Sela crumpled to the floor, and he turned to Data in amazement. He had certainly tried to teach others that maneuver in the past, including his former captain, James Kirk. No one had ever quite mastered the technique, and Spock had not attempted to impart the knowledge to anyone in decades.

But the android had accomplished the task, and apparently only from watching Spock's own performance of the pinch on the Romulan guard. It was a brilliant assimilation of the procedure. Rarely had he seen anything quite so remarkable.

"Not bad," was all Spock said, and they began to figure out how they could get out of that office and into the east wing of the building.

As soon as the Vulcan ships—which they now knew were carrying an invasion force—were within hailing range, Riker ordered Worf to open a channel. Then he stepped toward the viewscreen.

"I am Commander William Riker of the Federation starship *Enterprise*. Identify yourself."

The viewscreen flickered and then the image of a smiling Romulan captain appeared. "Commander, I am Danut of Romulus. We are a peace envoy, on our way to Vulcan. Our mission is an historic one. We welcome your congratulations."

Amazing. Riker never ceased to be astonished the way some people can look you straight in the eye, smile at you, and lie. "I assume you're hoping we didn't hear Ambassador Spock's message, sir. Unfortunately, we know you are an invasion force. You are occupying stolen Vulcan vessels, which we must retrieve. Please set a course for Starbase 314. We are prepared to tow you with a tractor beam if you do not comply."

The smile froze on Danut's face. "You are mistaken. Ambassador Spock's message was an announcement of the impending reunification talks between Romulus and Vulcan. You have no legitimate grounds to interfere, Commander. I suggest you fall back."

"We will be within tractor range in three minutes. Change course now or suffer the consequences."

Danut's face flushed darkly, and his fury crackled over the viewscreen. "We are armed, Commander. We will not hesitate to fire in order to preserve this historic mission."

"You are no match for the *Enterprise* and you know it," snapped Riker. "Now change course, bearing two-one-seven, mark zero-zero-seven."

Suddenly Riker saw a Romulan aide hurry to Danut's side and whisper something to him. At about the same time, Worf announced, "Vulcan defense vessels are also responding."

So Spock's announcement had reached his home planet, and ships were rushing to prevent the

Romulan force from invading their planet. Riker watched as Danut's visage grew dark and glowering. "We have no further business, Commander," he said, and the viewscreen returned to a starfield.

"Sir," said Worf, "the Romulan force is retreating toward the Neutral Zone."

"Oh, no," said Riker. "They're not taking those Vulcan ships home with them." He realized he felt downright proprietary about those Vulcan ships. Those were *his* Vulcan ships. He'd invested himself in them—well, one—and now he wasn't going to see some arrogant Romulan take them back across the Neutral Zone.

"Change course. Pursue the Vulcan ships."

"Sir, they have gone to warp eight. They will be within the Neutral Zone in minutes."

"Acknowledged, Mister Worf. Warp nine. Proceed."

Riker saw Worf and Geordi exchange looks, and knew they were thinking that he was playing it close to the edge. Well, so be it. He wasn't going to let go now, after all this. He was willing to risk an unauthorized entry into the Neutral Zone in order to apprehend the Romulan force and reclaim the ships that he was sure had been stolen from Federation depots. He had come too far to quit now.

Picard would have admitted that he was nervous about making this next maneuver work. But he had no better alternatives to offer, and so he agreed they had to take this chance if they were to get out of Sela's office and escape the Irnilt.

The greatest source of his apprehension was that

they could not carry disruptors. They would be unarmed, and consequently dependent on the cleverness of their scheme. There was no contingency plan; either this worked or they would be easily recaptured.

And so he stood with Spock and Data as two security guards entered the room and Sela rose to greet them. She gestured toward her prisoners disdainfully. "These fools are unwilling to talk. Take them to the underground tunnel in the east wing. Turn them over to Semeth. He may be more persuasive."

The guards nodded obediently and gestured Spock, Picard, and Data toward the door. Sela's men carried disruptors at their sides but did not draw them. Picard was sure they felt confident that there was little the prisoners could do within the well-guarded confines of the Irnilt.

And so the small band proceeded out of Sela's office and into the marble halls of the magnificent edifice. Remembering the oppressive streets at the ground level of Dartha, Picard was repulsed by the display of opulence here in the governmental building. The materials were lavish and costly, every detail exquisitely carried out. This was a bipartite world, the powerful existing almost literally above the substructure of the weak and impoverished.

They entered a cubicle not unlike the turbolifts on the *Enterprise* and began a dizzying journey down, sideways, and up again. Picard tried to estimate the time that had passed since they left the office. At some point, the real Sela would regain consciousness from the Vulcan pinch, and realize she had once again been the victim of Data's holographic expertise. She and her guards had lain unconscious behind that false wall, and could waken at any moment. If that happened before they were safely out of the building, they were doomed.

The cubicle finally came to a rest and doors slid open. The group exited to find themselves in a cavernous black corridor that reminded Picard of the caves he had recently visited with members of the unification movement. He had the sense that they were very deeply underground; all sound seemed muffled, and kekogen lights provided the only illumination.

They walked for some minutes through a labyrinth of passages, twisting and turning, until he had lost any sense of direction. He knew the maze had been planned for exactly that purpose; those who descended into these lonely depths were not intended to find their way out.

Picard stumbled slightly and paused briefly, unsure of his footing. "Keep walking," ordered one of the guards brusquely. Picard turned slightly toward him. "I'm having trouble breathing," he gasped. He bent over, drawing ragged breaths of air; a wheeze escaped him. He crumpled to the ground.

The guards were not fools. They did not rush to help him. They stood alertly at a distance as Spock and Data bent over Picard. Finally Spock rose and announced, "He cannot get up."

"Then carry him," came the terse reply.

"I am old. I do not have the physical strength."

The guard jerked his head toward Data. "Then you do it."

Data bent to Picard and then, as the captain's lips began moving, put his ear close to Picard's mouth. Then he rose.

"The captain is losing consciousness. He greatly

fears torture. He is willing to tell you what information he has, but he cannot speak above a whisper."

"It's a ruse," cautioned one of the guards.

Data shrugged. "I would not want to face Commander Sela with the news that the prisoner has died without having revealed what he knows—and all because you were afraid to listen to him."

The guards exchanged glances. One nodded to the other, and both drew their disruptors.

The first guard got to his knees and leaned in close to Picard. "There is a Federation spy among you," he whispered, "at the uppermost levels of the Romulan hierarchy."

Picard saw the guard look up toward his compatriot and nod. Then he leaned down again.

"His name," began Picard, "his name . . . his name is . . ." he began to wheeze again. The guard bent nearer still. "The name of the spy is—"

Had it not been for Data's speed, the rest could never have happened. Data was able to whirl and advance on the guard holding the disruptor so quickly that he literally had no idea what had happened.

At the same time, Spock pinched the neck of the guard listening to Picard.

A split second later, both guards lay unconscious from the pinch, and Picard and Data held their disruptors. There had been brief consideration of vaporizing the guards, rather than risk their recovering consciousness too soon, but none of the men could bring themselves to do it. Now, they looked back down the twisting maze of corridors through which they had been led. They needed the east-wing exit—but where was it?

"I think this way," said Picard, pointing to a passageway branching off to his right.

"I would have said this direction," countered Spock, pointing to the left.

"Forgive me, Captain, Ambassador," said Data mildly. "But if we are to get out of the Irnilt, you will have to rely on me."

And he began striding down the corridor straight ahead. Spock and Picard exchanged glances, and then, without a moment's hesitation, followed Data.

The *Enterprise* had penetrated well into the Neutral Zone before it overtook the three Vulcan/Romulan ships. The smaller vessels were no match for the Starfleet ship on any level—speed, sophistication, or firepower. Riker felt sure he could help the Romulans see reason; to do other than follow his directive was to risk dire consequences.

The Vulcan defense vessels, dispatched from the planet, had stopped at the Neutral Zone. Their only purpose was to prevent the Romulans from invading their system; if the encroaching force was in retreat, they had no reason to pursue.

And perhaps Riker should have followed the same logic. There was none to his present actions, a fact of which he was well aware.

But something drew him forward. He would listen to its urging now, and question it later.

"Visual range, Commander," said Worf, indicating that they had all but overtaken the fleeing Romulans.

"On screen," said Riker, preparing to engage Danut once more. He was wholly unprepared for what happened next.

Geordi saw it first, reacting from his sensors. "A

Romulan warbird, Commander. Decloaking alongside the Vulcan ships."

And now the quartet of ships sprang into relief on the viewscreen—the three small Vulcan vessels and the looming, ominous warbird that shimmered into sight next to them.

"Red alert," said Riker, and the lights flashed scarlet on the bridge.

A warbird was a very different story from the Vulcan craft. The Romulan D'Deridex class ship was as large and as powerful as the *Enterprise,* and as well armed. They would be at a standoff if it came to battle.

Riker's command was to Worf. "Advise the warbird to withdraw and leave the Vulcan ships where they are."

But Worf's response confirmed Riker's fears: "The warbird is powering up its forward disruptor array."

So it meant to attack. They were all violating treaty conditions by being within the Neutral Zone; here, there were no legal protections, no sanctions. It was unauthorized entry by all parties—and the devil take the hindmost.

"Ready phasers," said Riker grimly.

The warbird emitted a fierce salvo of its disruptors. And another. And another.

But to Riker's astonishment, the weapons fire was directed right at the Vulcan ships. One by one, they shuddered with the impact of the massive disruptor barrage; they discharged small bursts of burning gases into space; white fire crackled into an inferno that enveloped them.

And then they exploded.

The bridge crew of the *Enterprise* watched in awe as

the Vulcan ships ruptured, spewing matter. It was the ultimate fireworks display, a colorful, orgasmic array of burning metal and flesh, which catapulted flaming wreckage into the cold eternal night of space.

The warbird recloaked.

On the bridge of the *Enterprise,* the crew watched in stunned silence. Finally, Geordi spoke, and his voice sounded strangely harsh. "There were over two thousand Romulan troops on those ships," he said.

There was silence again.

"They destroyed their own invasion force," added Troi, as though trying to explain it to herself.

"Rather than let them be taken prisoner," offered Riker, seeking reason in an unreasonable act.

There was another quiet respite, then Riker spoke, quite softly. "Stand down red alert. Set a new course. Take us out of the Neutral Zone."

And the ship wheeled and turned away from the still burning carnage the Romulans had brought to bear upon their own people.

D'Tan had lain in wait for several hours in the rough *wagi* brush that provided camouflage and a clear view of the cave opening. He felt numb with shock and grief; the awful loss his people had suffered had not yet registered with him fully.

He still didn't know if his parents were alive or dead. Their rooms at the Taka were empty, and though he had searched through all the makeshift hospitals and shelters where the dazed survivors of Krocton segment were trying to care for their own, he had not found them.

They might have been killed in that first awful

slaughter on the streets. Or they might have been taken prisoner. If so, D'Tan doubted that he would ever see them again. He hoped they had died on the streets; to lose them would be terrible, but it would be preferable to imagining what they might be going through at the hands of Neral's guards.

A few of their number had regrouped at the cavern, and then decided immediately that they must not meet there again; they could expect periodic raids, and the location of the cave was compromised.

D'Tan had been posted as a lookout, to waylay any of their number who might mistakenly seek sanctuary there, and to be alert for security guards who might want to pay a return visit close on the heels of the first sweep.

He peered down the long road leading to Dartha. It was rough country out here, craggy and barren, with only this thorny native bush as covering. In the distance, the towering structures of the city rose like a dark growth of sinister crystal spires. D'Tan looked toward the skies, usually gray with volcanic particulates, and actually saw patches of blue beyond the haze. He wondered if ever he would sail those heavens toward Vulcan, as he had longed all his life to do.

He thought he spotted movement on the road. Tensing, he crouched lower in the brush. Was it the guards? Or dazed survivors of the Krocton massacre? He strained to make out the figures as they made their way up the road toward the caves.

When he realized who they were, D'Tan's heart leapt, and he could not contain himself. He burst out of the *wagi* brush, the thorns tearing at his clothes and skin, but he was oblivious. He went running, hard as he could, toward the advancing trio. Hope was pounding in his heart once more, and he felt the wind on his face and his feet pounding on the hard Romulan clay.

It felt good to be running again.

Picard saw the lithe figure coming at them, waving and shouting. He could not restrain a smile as he saw the child D'Tan fling himself into Spock's arms, hugging him and crying with joy and relief. Spock looked faintly embarrassed by this indulgent display of emotion, but he tolerated it patiently from the young boy.

Within half an hour, D'Tan had led them to a new range of rocky hills, and another subterranean cavern. They descended through a slippery passageway of loose shale, unsure of footing, clutching for support against the damp walls. There were no kekogen lights here; D'Tan carried a palm beacon that provided the only source of light.

But soon they emerged into a chamber lit by portable lamps, and saw a group of Romulan citizens —the small core of survivors of the dreadful massacre.

"Pardek never saw these caves," explained D'Tan. "It's safe, they won't find us here."

Picard's gaze swept over the people in the cavern. Some looked stunned and abstracted; all carried the grim look of those who have been witness to butchery. Many were wounded, and wore makeshift bandages on various parts of their body.

But there was an undeniable spirit that radiated from them, an unquenchable quality of endurance. These people had survived; more importantly, they had not lost hope. Their strength and determination hung in the air like a palpable presence.

"What will you do now?" Picard asked simply.

A young woman spoke immediately. "What we've always done. Continue to teach. Pass on the ideals to a new generation. Work for the day when new thoughts may be spoken aloud."

Picard glanced toward Spock, saw him listening to the young woman with intent, saw him glance toward D'Tan, whose eager face shone from the crowd.

"The Federation will welcome that day," Picard assured the young woman.

"Captain," reminded Data, "we will need to reach our transport site within an hour."

Picard nodded and as they began to move away from the others, he felt Spock touch his arm. Picard turned and looked into the ambassador's eyes, and suddenly he knew what Spock was about to say.

"I will not be coming with you."

Picard wanted to protest, wanted to show him how illogical such a decision would be. It was clear that Spock should come with them to the transport site, be beamed onto the Klingon ship, and return to Vulcan, where he would live out his years in safety and comfort, revered by his countrymen and all the people of the Federation.

It was clear that's what Picard should say. But he did not.

"The reason for my coming here has never been more clear, Captain," Spock continued. "The union of the Romulan and Vulcan peoples will not be achieved by politics. Or by diplomacy. But it will be achieved."

Spock moved away from him, pacing restlessly, formulating his thoughts. Picard's mind flashed back to their first meeting in the other caves, in what seemed a lifetime ago. The two men had been instantly in conflict, each of them stubbornly maintaining his position and assuming the other would back down.

Had that been only a few days ago?

"The answer has been here in front of us all the time," Spock went on. "An inexorable evolution toward a Vulcan philosphy has already begun. Like the first Vulcans, these people are struggling to find a new enlightenment. It may take decades, even centuries, for them to reach it. But they will. And I must help."

Picard studied the grave face, the penetrating eyes. "I have learned," he said finally, "that it is useless to argue with you once your mind is set."

"Not at all, Captain," retorted Spock. "I have in fact found our arguments quite useful. Almost as useful as those I had with my father."

Picard paused only briefly before he suggested, "Would you be surprised to learn that he found them equally valuable?"

Another long moment, and Picard could only imagine what was going on inside Spock's mind, but when he spoke, it was in the voice of a man who has achieved resolution. "Ironically, Captain, you may have known Sarek better than his own son did. My father and I never chose to meld."

And in that simple statement there lay a lifetime's relationship, of love felt and not expressed, of hurt and anger and pride, of arguments, accusations, of good deeds and mishaps, a century of tangled experiences and emotions never acknowledged. Therein lay the tragedy of Spock and his father.

Picard did not hesitate. "I would offer you the chance to touch what he shared with me."

Spock nodded, and extended his hand toward Picard's face. The strong, supple fingers pressed on his cheek, and once again Picard felt the wondrous blending of two spirits. His mind whirled, emotions reeled in tumultuous cacophony; images of his father, of rain-swept vineyards and sunny fields, of Spock and Sarek through all the times of tortured love they felt for each other, the strife and agony—all tumbled within him, joining, blending, transforming one into the other. It was overpowering, it was unbearable, the heightened sensations too vivid, too intense. . . . Ancient planets . . . French meadows ripe in yellow sunlight . . . Amanda giving birth . . . bitter cold . . . mechanized violation of the body and mind . . . fury . . . red mountains and withering deserts . . . the fatal bravery of a loyal pet . . . Perrin, Perrin, aching need . . . the aspiration to go forth. . . . What more is out there? What adventures yet remain? . . . Stars streaking, blurred . . . longing . . . sons and fathers . . . fathers and sons . . .

He stared into Spock's eyes, and Spock into his. Anguish bled away, serenity prevailed.

Unification.

The First Star Trek: The Next Generation
Hardcover Novel!

STAR TREK®
THE NEXT GENERATION™

REUNION

Michael Jan Friedman

Captain Pickard's
past and present
collide on board the
U.S.S. *Enterprise*™

POCKET
BOOKS

Available in Hardcover
from Pocket Books

444-01